PRAISE FOR *IN CALABRIA*

"A novella about love in a world of hardship, loss, magic, and recovery. Beagle's unicorns have never been more bewitching, impossible, and genuine. I cherished every page."
—Gregory Maguire, author of *Wicked* and *After Alice*

"Peter S. Beagle is a master of the magical, but also of the little details of day to day existence that root his characters in the soil, sweat and everyday breezes of their worlds, and make the magical all the more magical when it touches them. It's deep and powerful magic that stirs things to life in the gentle fable of *In Calabria*, but what it stirs—greed, peril, beauty, grief, love, publicity, sorrow, poetry and more—are very much matters of the human heart. Beagle once again explores the magic within us and the magic around us, and does it in unmatched style."
—Kurt Busiek, author of *Astro City* and *The Avengers*

★ "Acclaimed fantasist Beagle (*Summerlong*) sets this charming, lyrical tale of unicorns and love on a poor little hillside farm in the toe of boot-shaped Italy, where 47-year-old Claudio Bianchi scratches out a meager existence for himself, old dog Garibaldi, goat Cherubino, three cows, a pig, and three cats. Claudio writes poetry, too, and one day a golden-white unicorn appears to him as a gentle reminder of the freedom animals and humans have lost. The unicorn becomes the one miracle of Claudio's life— and the ultimate tourist attraction. He protects her as best he can from hordes of reporters, television crews and helicopters, animal rights activists, yearning yokels, and even the Calabrian 'Ndràngheta mob. After Claudio helps the unicorn deliver her colt, his heart, frozen by an earlier tragedy, warms to Giovanna, the intrepid 20-ish sister of the postman. Neatly playing the strictures of Claudio's simple rural life against the shimmering wildness of the unicorn, Beagle's kindly fable shows how a man who seems to have nothing can really have everything— with just a touch of magic."

—*Publishers Weekly*, starred review

"*In Calabria* is smart, heart-touching, specific and metaphoric; at the same time, lyrical, stunning. And any one who writes or wants to write, or loves to read, should read it."

—Jane Yolen, author of *The Devil's Arithmetic*

"Peter Beagle weaves his trademark magic deep in the Italian countryside, using threads of the everyday and the fantastical: poetry and pigs, Mafia bosses and terrible beauty, love and rage, the sacred born of the profane. *In Calabria* holds the power to transform, like the touch of the unicorn at its heart."
—Laurie R. King, author of the Mary Russell series (*The Beekeeper's Apprentice*)

"What a wondrous gift it is to have a new unicorn story from Peter S. Beagle! *In Calabria* is both elegant and earthy, with a slow build of wonder, and then tension, and then growing dread that propels the reader inexorably toward the miraculous conclusion. Once again Peter Beagle demonstrates why he is one of the greatest fantasy writers of all time!"
—Bruce Coville, author of *The Unicorn Chronicles*

"For me, Peter S. Beagle is one of the essential voices in American literature, so essential that I approach each new book he writes not only with excitement but also with trepidation. Can he possibly do it again? Today I read *In Calabria* from cover to cover. He does it again."
—Kevin Brockmeier, bestselling author of *The Brief History of the Dead*

"*In Calabria* is a gorgeous story shaped with elegant prose and stunning imagery. . . . It is a unicorn story. It is a coming of age story. It is a story of forgiveness and a story of love. *In Calabria* will speak to each and every reader that ventures through its pages."
—*So Many Books, So Little Time*

PRAISE FOR PETER S. BEAGLE

"One of my favorite writers."
—Madeleine L'Engle, author of *A Wrinkle in Time*

"Peter S. Beagle illuminates with his own particular magic such commonplace matters as ghosts, unicorns, and werewolves. For years a loving readership has consulted him as an expert on those hearts' reasons that reason does not know."
—Ursula K. Le Guin, author of *A Wizard of Earthsea* and *The Left Hand of Darkness*

"The only contemporary to remind one of Tolkien."
—*Booklist*

"Peter S. Beagle is (in no particular order) a wonderful writer, a fine human being, and a bandit prince out to steal readers' hearts."
—Tad Williams, author of *Tailchaser's Song*

"[Beagle] has been compared, not unreasonably, with Lewis Carroll and J. R. R. Tolkien, but he stands squarely and triumphantly on his own feet."
—*Saturday Review*

"Not only one of our greatest fantasists, but one of our greatest writers, a magic realist worthy of consideration with such writers as Márquez, Allende, and even Borges."
—*The American Culture*

"Before all the endless series and shared-world novels, Beagle was there to show us the amazing possibilities waiting in the worlds of fantasy, and he is still one of the masters by which the rest of the field is measured."
—Lisa Goldstein, author of *The Red Magician*

"Peter S. Beagle would be one of the century's great writers in any arena he chose."
—Edward Bryant, author of *Cinnabar*

PRAISE FOR *SUMMERLONG*

"Beagle's novel *Summerlong* is a lovely, tantalizing read that moves through a finely detailed, familiar world into a tale as old and as urgent as language."
—Patricia A. McKillip, author of *The Riddle-Master of Hed* and *Dreams of Distant Shores*

"*Summerlong* is beautiful in its love for our messy complexity; for the first step into cold water, for the death that lets us grow again, and the ways we learn to love each other—and ourselves—wiser and better."
—Leah Bobet, author of *An Inheritance of Ashes*

"Best-selling fantasy-author Beagle crafts a tantalizing picture of an atypical Pacific Northwestern couple whose lives are interrupted by myth and mystery."
—*Booklist*

"In his first new novel in more than a decade, Beagle creates an intimate drama . . . a beautifully detailed fantasy."
—*Kirkus*

PRAISE FOR *THE LAST UNICORN*

"*The Last Unicorn* is the best book I have ever read. You need to read it. If you've already read it, you need to read it again."
—Patrick Rothfuss, author of *The Name of the Wind* and *The Wise Man's Fear*

"Almost as if it were the last fairy tale, come out of lonely hiding in the forests of childhood, *The Last Unicorn* is as full of enchantment as any of the favorite tales readers may choose to recall."
—*St. Louis Post-Dispatch*

"*The Last Unicorn* is one of the true classics of fantasy, ranking with Tolkien's *The Hobbit*, Le Guin's *Earthsea Trilogy*, and Lewis Carroll's *Alice in Wonderland*. Beagle writes a shimmering prose-poetry, the voice of fairy tales and childhood."
—*Amazon.com*

Also by Peter S. Beagle

Fiction
A Fine & Private Place (1960)
The Last Unicorn (1968)
Lila the Werewolf (1969)
The Folk of the Air (1986)
The Innkeeper's Song (1993)
The Unicorn Sonata (1996)
Tamsin (1999)
A Dance for Emilia (2000)
The Last Unicorn: The Lost Version (2007)
Strange Roads (with Lisa Snellings Clark, 2008)
Return (2010)
Summerlong (2016)

Short story collections
Giant Bones (1997)
*The Rhinoceros Who Quoted Nietzsche and Other
Odd Acquaintances* (1997)
The Line Between (2006)
*Your Friendly Neighborhood Magician: Songs and
Early Poems* (2006)
We Never Talk About My Brother (2009)
Mirror Kingdoms: The Best of Peter S. Beagle (2010)
Sleight of Hand (2011)

Nonfiction

*I See By My Outfit: Cross-Country by Scooter,
an Adventure* (1965)
The California Feeling (with Michael Bry, 1969)
The Lady and Her Tiger (with Pat Derby, 1976)
The Garden of Earthly Delights (1982)
In the Presence of Elephants (1995)

As editor

Peter S. Beagle's Immortal Unicorn
(with Janet Berliner, 1995)
The Secret History of Fantasy (2010)
The Urban Fantasy Anthology (with Joe R.
Lansdale, 2011)

In Calabria
PETER S. BEAGLE

IN CALABRIA

PETER S. BEAGLE

TACHYON | SAN FRANCISCO

Interior and cover design by Elizabeth Story

Tachyon Publications LLC
1459 18th Street #139
San Francisco, CA 94107
415.285.5615
www.tachyonpublications.com
tachyon@tachyonpublications.com

Series Editor: Jacob Weisman
Project Editor: Rachel Fagundes

ISBN 13: 978-1-61696-248-7

First Edition: 2017
9 8 7 6 5 4 3 2 1

Printed in the United States by Maple Press

For Ayesha L. Collins,
brave and beautiful,
always,
even when weary and sad

"The whole trouble with your farm," Romano Muscari said, "is that it is too far uphill for the American suntanners, and too low for the German skiers. Location is everything."

"The trouble with my farm," Claudio Bianchi growled through his heavy, still-black mustache, "is that, no matter where it is located, the *postino* somehow manages to find his way out here twice a week. Rain or shine. Mail or no mail."

Romano grinned. "Three times a week, starting next month. New government." He was barely more than half Bianchi's age, but a friend of long enough standing to take no offense at anything the Calabrese said to him. Romano himself had been born in the Abruzzi, and in a bad mood Bianchi would inform him that his name suited him to perfection, since he spoke like a Roman. It was not meant as a compliment. Now he leaned on the little blue van that served him as a mail truck and continued, "No, I am serious. Whichever way you look—down toward Scilla, Tropea, up to Monte Sant'Elia, you are simply in the wrong place to attract the tourists. I grieve to mention this, but it is unlikely that you will ever be able to convert this farm into a celebrated tourist attraction. No bikinis, no ski lifts and charming snow outfits. A great pity."

"A blessing. What do I need with tourists, when I have you to harass me with useless advertisements, and Domenico down in the *villaggio* to sell me elderly chickens, and that thief Falcone to cheat me on the price of my produce, when I could get twice as much in Reggio—"

"If that truck of yours could get even halfway to Reggio—"

"It is a fine truck—Studebaker, American-made, a classic. All it needs is to have the transmission repaired, which I will not have Giorgio Malatesta do, because he uses cheap parts from Albania. Meanwhile, I endure what I must. *Whom* I must." He squinted dourly at the young postman. "Do you not have somewhere else to be? Truly? On a fine day like today?"

"Well . . ." Romano stretched out the word thoughtfully. "I did tell Giovanna that I would give her a driving lesson. She is learning my route, you know, in case of emergencies. Such as me actually needing to sleep."

"Your sister? Your sister is not yet old enough to drive a motorcycle!"

Romano shook his head slowly and sorrowfully. "The saddest thing in this world is to watch the decline of a once-great mind. You can no longer even remember that Giovanna will be twenty-three years old next month." He rolled his eyes, regarding the sky accusingly. "She cannot live with me forever. People will talk. Once she graduates, she will most likely move in with her friend Silvana, until she can find work and a place of her own. Just as you will undoubtedly need a quiet room where you can sit untroubled all day and write your poetry. Food and calming medications will be brought to you periodically." He caressed the graying muzzle of Garibaldi, Bianchi's theoretical watchdog, and glanced warily sideways at the short, barrel-chested farmer. "Have you written any nice poems lately, by the way?"

"I do not write poetry. As you know. I sometimes—*sometimes*—read poetry to my cows, because they seem to like it. But it is not *my* poetry, never my poetry. I read them Leopardi, Pavese, Pozzi, Montale—poets of some size, some humanity, poets perhaps to make my cows understand what a thing it is to be a man or a woman." He cleared his throat and spat neatly into a tuft of weeds, startling Sophia, the stub-tailed three-legged cat, who was stalking a sparrow. "Now even if I *did* write poetry, I would never dream of reciting it to the cows. They have been raised to have taste. I would be shamed."

"Admirable modesty. Truly admirable." Romano clucked his tongue approvingly. "Well, I must tear myself away from this peaceable kingdom, or my flyers will not go through, and poor Giovanna will wait in vain for her lesson." He patted the blue van's left front fender, as he always did on getting into it; when Claudio mocked him as a superstitious peasant, Romano would reply serenely that the routine was merely to reassure himself that the fender remained attached. Starting the engine, he leaned out and spoke over its raspy hiccup. "One day you will see that girl driving this machine up the hill to your door, just as I do. She is a very quick learner."

Bianchi snorted like a shotgun. "She is too young. She will always be too young. You are too young." He stepped back, raising a hand in a gesture that might conceivably have meant farewell, but could just as easily have been directed at an annoying gnat.

Romano and his sister had barely started school when Bianchi inherited the rambling farm west of Siderno, north of Reggio, from a second cousin on his grandfather's side whom he could never remember meeting. The Bianchis of southern Calabria as a group generally disliked one another, but they disliked outsiders even more, and there was no question of selling off the farm as long as there was some splinter of the family tree to take it over. It was still referred to locally as "the Greek's place," because a Bovesian relative of some generations back had supposedly spoken a dialect that contained some words and phrases of the ancient Griko tongue. Claudio Bianchi had his doubts, as he did about most things.

He was forty-seven years old: short, barrel-chested, and broad-shouldered, like most of his family, like most of the men he had known all his life. His black hair was increasingly patched with gray, but remained as thick as ever, and his skin was the color of the earth he worked every day in the sun of the *mezzogiorno*. The lines around his eyes were as harsh as the land, far more likely to have been inscribed by weariness, anger, and bone-born skepticism than by laughter; but the large eyes themselves were deep brown, and their wary warmth should have had no place in the heavy-boned face of a Calabrese farmer possessed of no illusion that God and his angels ever came this far south. Bianchi had been embarrassed by his eyes on a few odd occasions.

The afternoon was sunny but chill, unusual for the region, even in November. Bianchi had noticed animals he saw every day, from his three cats and the old goat Cherubino to the neighboring weasels and foxes to rabbits and caterpillars, growing heavier coats than normal; he had had to start heating his cow barn at night, a month or more early, and begin swaddling his outdoor faucets and hoses—even the Studebaker's engine block— against the cold. He growled often to Romano, or Domenico, or to Michaelis the village innkeeper— who really *was* Greek—that one might as well be living in England or Denmark. Or in Pedraces Bolzano, if it came to that. Bianchi tended to disapprove of all of Italy north of Milano.

In fact, however, he rather enjoyed this odd cold snap, or climate change, or whatever it was. It did no harm to his cabbages, kale, onions, scallions, eggplants, and potatoes, long since harvested and sold to that thief Falcone, nor—as long as the rain was not excessive—to the dwindling hillside vineyard that he kept up out of pure stubbornness when he had let so much else crumble and blow away, and it was a positive benefit to his dormant apple trees, ensuring crisp tartness come spring. If Gianetta, Martina, and Lucia, his three cows, had not been put to stud in more than a year— and could die as virginal as Giovanna Muscari, as long as that shameless pirate Cianelli kept demanding such outlandish fees for the use of his reportedly Friesian bull—still their milk kept coming, and kept the cats and the cheesemaking Rosmini brothers happy. If the old house was little more than kitchen, bedroom, bath, a bit of a parlor, and an attic long since closed off and still, nevertheless it held the heat from his oven and his fireplace better than a larger one would have done; if the nights were dark and silent, the better for thinking and smoking his pipe in peace. And for writing poetry.

For Romano was quite right about that. Claudio Bianchi did write poetry, at highly irregular intervals during his solitary daily life as a farmer in the toe of the Italian boot. Few of his acquaintances—Romano again excepted—knew that he had finished high school before going to work; or that, despite both of these circumstances, he had never lost his childhood love of reading poems, and in time trying to imitate them. He had no vanity about this, no fantasies of literary celebrity: he simply took pleasure in putting words in order, exactly as he laid out seedlings in the spring, and tasting them afterward, as he tasted fresh new scallions or ripe tomatoes, or smelled mint or garlic on his hands. He never thought of his poems as being *about* anything: they came when they came, sometimes resembling what he saw and touched and thought all day—sometimes, to his surprise, becoming visions of what his father's days and nights might have been like, or Romano's, or even those of Cianelli's aging bull. He would say a coming poem over to himself while he was repairing the Studebaker or his tractor, repainting the barn, or adding red peppers to his dinner of sautéed *melanzane* eggplant. They came when they came, and when they were finished, he knew. Nothing else—as he often thought—was ever truly completed; there was always something else to be added, repaired, or corrected to make it right. But when a poem was done, it was done. There was satisfaction in this.

As there was in living in the old house where the dirt road ran out, inhabiting a life that he was perfectly aware could have been a nineteenth-century life, if one ignored the electricity, gasoline, and the telephone he often went weeks at a time without using. Sometimes, when the reception was not too erratic, he watched news broadcasts on the little television set he had accepted in payment for helping to recover a neighbor's escaped black pigs (come to visit his own half-dozen) and then repairing the gap in the fence through which they had made their getaway. He could not remember the last movie he had seen, nor the last doctor; and he was more likely to whistle ancient Neapolitan *canzone* about his work than operatic arias. His teeth were excellent; he most often cut his own hair, washed and mended his own clothes, and quite enjoyed his own simple cooking. He knew something of sorrow, remembered joy, and devoutly hoped—as much as he consciously hoped for anything other than proper allotments of sunshine and rainfall—never again to encounter either of those two old annoyances. Asked, he would have grumbled, "*Sono contento,*" if he bothered to respond to such intrusion at all.

The universe and Claudio Bianchi had agreed long ago to leave one another alone, and he was grateful, knowing very well how rare such a bargain is, and how rarely kept. And if he had any complaints, he made sure that neither the universe nor he himself ever knew of them.

The morning after Romano's last visit—he had few other regular callers, except for the one local policeman, *Tenente* Esposito, who was near retirement, and would sometimes stop by without notice for a cup of coffee with a dash of *grappa* in it, and two hours of complaining about his grown children—Bianchi stepped outside on a sunny, frosty morning, *the American scientists are right, something is changing*, determined to finish pruning his tottering grapevines before the *sirocco* blew in from Africa to deceive crops with its treacherous warmth. The Undertaker's Wind rasped his cheek, *late, it should have been blowing well before dawn.* He looked around for Cherubino, mildly surprised that the goat—a far more aggressive sentinel than Garibaldi—was not at the door to greet and challenge him, then bent to scratch the black cat Mezzanotte behind the ears. He straightened up and shrugged into his battered, beloved leather jacket, thinking, *there is a poem in this coat*—

stretched his arms pleasurably, yawned, scratched the back of his own shaggy neck, and saw the unicorn in his vineyard.

Cherubino was a little way from it, seemingly frozen in the attitude of a fawning acolyte: head bowed, front legs stretched out on the ground before him, as Bianchi had never seen the old goat. The unicorn ignored him in a courteous manner, moving with notable care around the fragile arbors, never touching the vines, but nibbling what weeds it could find on the cold ground. It was a kind of golden white, though its mane and tail—long and tufted, like a lion's tail—were slightly darker, as was the horn set high on its silken brow.

As Bianchi stared, it looked up, meeting his eyes with its own, which were dark but not black: more like the darkness of a pine forest in moonlight. It showed no alarm at his presence, nor even when he took his first slow step toward it; but when he asked, "What do you want?"—or tried to ask, because the words would not come out of his mouth—the unicorn was gone, as though it had never been there at all. He would indeed have taken it for an illusion, if Cherubino, anarchist and atheist like all goats, had not remained kneeling for some time afterward, before getting to his feet, shaking himself and glancing briefly at Bianchi before wandering off. Bianchi knew the truth then, and sat down.

He remained on his doorstep into the afternoon, hardly moving, not even thinking in any coherent pattern or direction: simply reciting his vision in his head, over and over, as he was accustomed to do when shaping one of his own poems. Garibaldi, who apparently had not even noticed the unicorn, came up and nuzzled his cheek, and Mezzanotte and Sophia in turn pressed themselves under his hands, seemingly more for comfort than caresses. Bianchi responded as always, but without speaking or looking at them. The sun was beginning to slip behind the Aspromonte Mountains before he stood up and walked out to his vineyard.

He did not bring his pruning shears with him, but only stood for a time—not long—staring at the faint cloven hoofprints in the still-near-frozen soil. Then he went back to the house and closed the door behind him.

At some distance, he was aware that he had eaten nothing at all that day, yet he was not at all hungry; in the same way he thought somewhere about opening the bottle of Melissa Gaglioppo that he had been saving most of the year for some unspecified celebration. In fact, he did nothing but sit all night at the wobbly kitchen table that served him as a desk, writing about what he had seen at sunrise. It was neither a poem, insofar as he could judge, nor any sort of journal entry, nor a letter, had there been anyone for him to write to. It was whatever it was, and he stayed at it and with it until Garibaldi scratched at the door to be let in, and brought him home from wherever he and the unicorn had been. He lay down on his bed then, slept not at all; and at last rose to stand in the doorway in his undershirt, looking out at the stubbly fields that comprised his fingernail scratching at the earth.

Not much for forty-seven years, Bianchi. You have let this place melt away under you for such a long time. When you are gone, it will all melt back into the earth, and who will even know you were here?

The moon was down, but its absence made the sky seem even brighter, crusted thickly with more stars than he was accustomed to seeing. The unicorn was in his melon patch, and Cherubino was again with it, this time close enough to touch noses with the creature. The goat's stubby tail was wagging in circles, as it habitually did in those uncommon moments of excitement over something other than eating. Bianchi was almost more astonished by the fact that Cherubino was taking the same care as the unicorn to avoid trampling any of the fragile vines than by the bright apparition pacing daintily among the husks of the melons that he faithfully planted for the deer, in appreciation for their leaving his tomatoes alone. He hardly dared to look at it directly, until the unicorn stamped a forefoot lightly, as though to attract his attention. There was no other sound in the night.

For a second time, Bianchi asked, "What do you want of me? Are you here to tell me something?" The unicorn only looked calmly back at him. Bianchi fought to clear his throat, finally managing to speak again. "Am I going to die?"

The unicorn made no response, but Cherubino bleated once, as though as to say, "And leave *me* here alone, at the mercy of the wolves and the weather, with nothing fresh-budded and tempting for me to eat? I should hope not, indeed!" The unicorn looked sideways at the goat, and there was a quick star-glint in one dark eye that Bianchi might have taken for humor, if he could have imagined unicorns sharing that particularly human attribute.

Bianchi walked toward it, taking one wary step at a time, as before. He said, more clearly now, "If I am to die, I must make some provision for the animals. Please tell me."

The unicorn met his eyes fully once more, and then vanished so swiftly that Bianchi would have, with time and determination, remembered it as a play of shadow and starlight, but for the single distant chime of a hoof on stone. He was left alone with Cherubino, who gave him one dismissive glance out of one slit yellow pupil, then fell to eating withered rinds. Bianchi said, "*Mal' occhio*, you know what you saw," and shooed him out of the melon patch.

But the unicorn returned that same day. Bianchi saw it as he was gathering the last windfall apples to pulp and dry for feed that, along with last summer's timothy hay, would keep the cows all winter. It seemed almost to be pacing the boundaries of his land, instinctively sensing and measuring them, for what purpose Bianchi could not imagine. There was no fear or apprehension in its bearing: it neither came closer than twenty feet or thereabouts, of its own accord, nor darted instantly away if he approached or addressed it. Its beauty struck him like a blow, even when he was not actually looking at it; with his back turned, his body still remained aware—not altogether comfortably, either—of the unicorn's nearness.

He did not dream of it when he went to bed that night, nor did Garibaldi rouse him. He did not need to see the cloven tracks by his doorway the next morning to know that the unicorn had been there.

It remained a constant presence on his land from that day forth, whether he happened to catch sight of it or not. Garibaldi accepted it from the first day, though he was too old and indolent to attend on it as worshipfully as Cherubino, while Sophia, Mezzanotte, and even the feral, near-wild Third Cat, whose true name he had never discovered, as one has to do with cats, trailed after it like watchful children, keeping their distance. The pigs ate and snuffled and drowsed, and tried their fence one more time; only the three cows, led out every day for air, manure production, and such cold grazing as there was, seemed at all tense or uncomfortable at sight of the stranger. They would kick up their heels and lumber clumsily away if the unicorn drew too near. The unicorn took no smallest notice of their behavior, clearly having something profoundly other on its mind. Bianchi's admittedly total ignorance of what that might possibly be was not made easier by his suspicion that Cherubino, the goat, knew.

Paradoxically, or perhaps not, this frustration did set him writing poetry with a furious energy that he had never before experienced. Not all of the poems were directly about the unicorn; not even when, sitting at his little kitchen table, he could see the horn glimmering like a firefly among his bare apple trees, or glowing on a far hillside at the edge of his land. He wrote from the point of view of Cherubino, or Third Cat, or a passing cloud, or the winter earth itself, warming to the light impress of the cloven hooves.

Unlike his usual way of working, which involved laborious crossing out, scribbling between lines, perpetual starting over, and patient, stubborn searching for better words, these new poems were written without a single backward glance—quite often without rereading. As he completed each one, he shoved it with the others into a rickety schoolroom desk inherited with the house. He gave them no titles; he never saw the point of doing so. If a poem did not tell you immediately what it was about, then, to Claudio Bianchi, it needed more help than a label was likely to provide.

The weather continued untypically cold, and more people than Bianchi complained about it. Michaelis's tourists, who tended to be hikers more than skiers, looked at the television reports and canceled long-established reservations by the busload. This in turn seriously affected the fortunes of Domenico the village wineseller, Dallessandro the butcher and plumber, Rossi the barber, Broglio the baker, and even Leonora Venucci, the ancient fortune-teller, palm-reader, medium-at-large, and respected full-service sibyl.

The rains came early that winter, and they came

savagely enough that Romano Muscari's blue van could not always struggle up the winding dirt road to deliver Bianchi's inconsequential mail. When he did manage the journey, Bianchi invariably made a point of assuring him of his gratitude for being spared their twice-weekly chats. "You always talked too much when you were a skinny little *ragazzo*, and it has only gotten worse with the years. When you are my age—if no one has strangled you before that time—you will be as impossible as your father, rest his soul. That man at least knew how to be quiet once in a while."

Romano would grin cheekily back at him, and even take the liberty of nudging his shoulder. "Poetry not going so well, *non e vero?*"

"I have told you, I do not write poetry. Go away, and take this dog's dinner of a post with you—and do not waste your time and mine bringing me travel brochures and information on how to lose weight, become rich, and buy property in Spain with my new wealth. And be careful going home on those bald tires, *ascoltame.* Do you hear?"

"You would miss me? You would be just a little distressed? Incommoded in the slightest degree?"

"Go away."

The unicorn was never in sight when the young postman visited; nor, for all the rain, did he once notice that the cloven prints near his habitual parking place were too small and clean to have been made by cows. The poems kept coming, as steadily and strangely as the downpours; and Bianchi did on occasion admit to himself that it was almost—*almost*—tempting at times to show or recite a couple of them to Romano. But this would inevitably mean revealing the existence of the unicorn as well—there was nothing symbolic or figurative about it in the poetry—and that Bianchi was not prepared to do for anyone. The creature had come to him of its own will, had chosen his rundown farm for its own reasons; if it had wanted to show itself to anyone else, it would surely have chosen to do so. He had no right to make choices for such a being, as though it were a vine to be pruned, a tree to be grafted, a dog to be put down when it grew too old to hunt. And besides . . . besides . . .

. . . it was *his* unicorn, and no one else's. He fought bitterly against that private confession, knowing perfectly well what it said of him. But Claudio Bianchi was an honest single man—*a long time now, and the best thing for both of us—*

with no one to answer to but himself. His sense of honor was his own; and if he knew that what he felt deeply was selfish and shameful, at least he knew it, and had no wish to pretend otherwise. *Is that what makes me write the poems? Perhaps so.*

Curiously, he saw the unicorn more often, and more closely, during the rains, though it never appeared to be seeking shelter from cold or dampness or wind. It did seem to him to be moving more purposefully, though he could not quite have said what he meant by that, and to be narrowing its search—if that was what it was—down to certain particular areas of his farm: the little apple orchard, for one, and a wide, shallow hollow within sight of his house, which always gathered water during such weather as this. He had tried potatoes there more than once, and turnips and rutabagas as well, but unfailingly lost them to rot, despite the partial protection of an eyebrow overhang of earth, held together by grass and the half-exposed roots of a dying chestnut tree.

The unicorn kept returning to those two places, lowering its head often, as though smelling the ground itself, testing its solidity with a forehoof, even prodding the chestnut with its horn, for no reason that Bianchi could comprehend. He caught cold twice that winter, trying not so much to follow the unicorn as to make sense of its wanderings on his land. "*Your land now,*" he said to it in a poem.

> *Your land, who can doubt it?*
> *as you reclaim all lands stolen*
> *from you*
> *by those whose only gift is for stealing beauty*
> *take it back from me now*
> *take it all back . . .*

Cherubino, accepting him as a fellow acolyte, often kept him company, as a younger Garibaldi might have done, often bumping his own horned head against him when he hesitated on a muddy path, uncertain of direction. Bianchi found this behavior slightly unnerving in an animal as self-willed as Cherubino, but when so much else was changing so fast, why not a goat? *For that matter, why should my cows, ten thousand years bred down from their wild ancestors to be slaughtered and eaten, forced to pull ploughs and produce milk for the children we slaughter in turn, have any reason to see in a unicorn anything but a poignant reminder of their own lost freedom? As do I, as do I, that is what all these new poems are about, and maybe all the others, long before, from the beginning. It is not the same thing, of course, but still it is.*

The unicorn neither avoided him nor came any closer than it ever had, even when he stood perfectly still, emptying his mind, as much as he could, of all thought, whether concerning poetry, farming, rain, cooking, or a beauty that hurt his heart beyond naming as pain. On occasion, without warning or conscious intent, everything in him seemed to focus entirely on the shining horn, as though the unicorn itself, and all around it—not merely his handful of hectares, but the far mountains and the tourist sea as well—had converged to that one bright, sharp point in the universe. He would stare at it until his eyes ached and watered, and his head drummed so that he always had to go back to the house and lie down. *I am past visitations. What do you want with me?*

He spoke those words aloud, into the air, having fallen into the habit of talking to the unicorn, whether it was present to his view or not. This was more than simply new for him—despite what he had told Romano, his speech to his animals never went beyond a command, a rebuke, or a nearly wordless murmur of affection—it actually frightened him to hear his own voice. *Once Uncle Vincenzo began talking to his chickens, everybody knew. The dog was one thing—but the chickens! Everybody knew then.* But this was different, surely—this was more like the poems, a way of finding out what he felt about things, telling himself the truth of what was before his eyes. That had to be different from Uncle Vincenzo.

"You are just as much out of place here as Romano says I am," he told the unicorn. "Either you belong in the highest ranges of the Aspromonte or the Pollino, where only the bravest climbers will catch a glimpse of you, and take you for a mountain sheep . . . or else you should be sporting in the magical woodlands of Tuscany, a legend out of the fairytales and the songs of the *podestà* troubadours. What can you imagine you are doing here, with no princes and dukes to hunt you, no noble ladies to embroider you—no one to do you honor but a tired, tired old farmer with his tired old dog and his cows and cats, and his *pazzo* goat? You have no business in poor, tired Calabria, and we both know it."

Another time, waving an ancient bulb-setter (daffodils were his one floral weakness) at the radiance in his potato field, he announced, "When the wind changes, and you smell the new moon and dance off over the hills and far away, the only heart broken around here will be the goat's. I want you to understand that. You are a miracle, yes, truly— the one miracle of my life—but miracles do not break the heart. Foolish, ridiculous things do that, songs do that, smells do that, everyday stupidities do that . . . not a unicorn leaving town. Pity poor Cherubino, not Bianchi." And after a few moments of kneeling and twisting the bulb-setter in the still-damp earth, he added, just as though the unicorn had spoken to him, "Of course I will miss you. When did I say that I would not miss you? But just so you know."

At times the unicorn actually appeared to be listening, even cocking its delicate, almost transparent ears to catch the words. Bianchi did not flatter himself that this was so—*I was practically a child, I liked it when Uncle Vincenzo used to tell me what the chickens said to him*—but he did rather enjoy hearing his gruff, unpracticed voice addressing someone other than a postman or a butcher, a

42

wineseller, a mechanic, and speaking of matters that he had not discussed with anyone but the poems since his earliest youth. To the unicorn he spoke without grooming or ordering his thoughts, without concern as to what such a creature might think of him—as though, in fact, to the oldest of old friends.

Perhaps that was the reason—for one pays at once the deepest and the most casual sort of attention to a friend of that standing—that it took him longer than it should have to connect the unicorn's increasing interest in the half-sheltered hollow near his house with a slight change in its graceful outline, visible only in a certain light, at a certain angle. He had been cleaning and sharpening a scythe outside his toolshed at the time, and actually cut a finger painfully when the realization finally descended upon him. The three words he uttered then clearly startled Cherubino, who had never heard them before. They were medieval in origin.

"You could have told me!" he growled at the goat. "You *knew*—you could have *said*!" Realizing the absurdity of this before the words were out of his mouth, he put the scythe away, wrapped his wounded finger in the tail of his shirt, and started directly toward the hollow, where the unicorn was visible in the lengthening twilight. It turned its head sharply at his approach, but did not flee him this particular time. He noticed signs that it had been pawing at the ground: not aggressively, but more like a cat or dog—or a bird, for that matter—making a nest.

"It is not the stupid goat's stupid fault," he muttered. "How could I not have known, *gran' disgraziato?*"

The unicorn made the first sound he had ever heard it make: neither a whinny nor a low, but something almost like the quiet ripple of water against a riverbank. Bianchi said in his most reasonable voice, "Why here? In the sweet name of Jesus and his mother Maria, not to mention every *porca miseria* saint in the *porca miseria* calendar, what can have possessed you to choose my *porca miseria* patch of dirt for your lying-in? Go to Palmi, by the sea—that's the place for someone like you. They have the *Casa della Cultura* there, they have the big *folklorico* museum, they will know how to honor a unicorn. What is there here for you . . . for you and your little one, but an old man living with a bunch of old animals on a forsaken hillside farm? There has been a great mistake. You must know this."

The unicorn made the soft sound again. It—*no, she, I must remember now*—abruptly folded her legs under herself and lay down, only to rise almost immediately and recommence lightly pawing the earth with her sharp, small hooves. Feeling utterly foolish, Bianchi asked, "Do you need me to help you? With my rake or something?" The unicorn looked at him. Bianchi said, "Then I will go now. If you do need me . . ."

He left the sentence unfinished, and turned away to walk to his house. He did not look back, nor did he stir out of doors that night, nor even steal to the window in hopes of spying on the unicorn, despite his knowledge that she was surely nowhere near ready to drop her . . . *colt? Or would it be fawn? Fawn, I suppose—but maybe not. Well, it will surely not be born soon. I can think about it?*

He wrote no poetry that night, not feeling the need at all. Nor did he feel like going to bed, but drifted through the little house, smiling at nothing, humming no song he recognized to himself. That time he did open the Melissa Gaglioppo, though he drank only sparingly, feeling a vague and primitive urge to use the wine to sanctify the spot where a unicorn had elected to give birth. *But she might very well be offended. I don't think unicorns are Christian beasts, but how would I know?*

But in the morning he went outside before he had even had his breakfast, and found the unicorn again lying down in the nest that she had scraped out for herself, having apparently lined it with grass—*or did Cherubino do that for her?* She rose swiftly as he approached, lowering her head in a warning attitude that he had never seen her take before. He halted immediately, not retreating, but holding up his hands, palm out, saying, "It's me, you know me." Which, when he thought about it, was probably true: without a word or a touch ever between them, the unicorn might very well know him better than anyone ever had. Bianchi said, "I will ask no more about your purpose, your choices. But if you should need me, I will be nearby."

And he kept his word, as best he could, being both a southern Calabrese and a Bianchi. From then on, he almost never left his land, except when absolutely necessary, to shop for food or tools in the village; or, once, to help out Romano when the mail van bogged down on a muddy curve. That time, he provided only the stubborn strength of his back and shoulders, and then hurried home without staying for talk, or for the *postino's* gratefully-proffered flask of *strega*.

It was not that he imagined the unicorn to be in danger if he were, in fact, not close at hand; his farm animals all gave birth without anyone's help, and seemed to prefer it so, as far as he could ever tell. But the little he knew about unicorns suggested that they mated seldom and gave birth even more rarely, and that she might indeed have some need of him when her time came. Over the years, he had developed a proper respect for Cherubino's goat-wisdom and Mezzanotte's mysterious feline reveries, but he had no great faith in their obstetrical skills.

From that point he began calling the unicorn *La Signora*, though only in his mind, and in the poems. It seemed more respectful.

Romano thought he had a woman, and was glad of it. "As long as we have known him," he said to his sister Giovanna, "which might as well be all our lives, he has been alone." He paused briefly, scratching his head. "Except for the little time when he was married. And I think he was alone even then."

Giovanna's heavy, dark eyebrows drew together. "I don't remember that at all—him being married. It is impossible to imagine."

"You were too little. I remember her, in a sort of way. She hugged us when she left." He was digging into his dinner, speaking to her with his mouth full. "He has lived like a hermit ever since. Up there in an empty house, growing sourer with the years, never seeing how much his solitude has changed him. A woman would tell him."

Giovanna shrugged. "He was always cranky— I never knew him any different. I liked him well enough when we were young, but I would not care to be the woman involved with him. Who, as you have never seen her, most likely does not exist at all." She rumpled his hair fondly. "Now you were always a romantic boy, and an extremely imaginative one. People do not change so much."

"Well, you tell me what you think when you see him next," Romano answered her, a bit pettishly. "You are good enough to drive my route right now—in a little while, when the roads are dryer, you will take over for me one day a week." He frowned heavily over the last of his *tonno cunzatu*, pretending to ponder. "I think it will be . . . Friday. Yes—every Friday you can deliver mail for me, gaining experience and making any number of new friends—"

"—while you pick up Tessa Moro on your motorcycle and whisk her off to wherever the two of you go on her Friday off. Very well, I will make your social life easier, because I am a good sister. And I will chat up Claudio Bianchi and get him to talk about *his* woman, if he has one—but if that stupid goat of his attacks me—"

"It is a very old goat, and no danger at all to you. And when you meet Bianchi's woman—"

"—*if* I meet her—"

"—I want you to study her as you are forever studying my Tessa—"

"—I *like* your Tessa a great deal, more or less—"

"—then you can tell me if you think she will make him happy." Setting his dinner plate in the sink, Romano turned to put his hands on his sister's shoulders. "Because I would like him to be happy. I really would."

Giovanna patted his cheek. "We will see. Perhaps I can persuade him to read me some of the poetry you tell me he writes. That would be at least interesting."

Romano shook his head decidedly. "I have never been able to make him show me even one poem. That won't happen."

"We will see," Giovanna said.

The unicorn continued to show few of the obvious signs of pregnancy as the weeks passed. Claudio Bianchi had no idea of how long such a gestation should normally take: he could only go by the gradual rounding of her sides, which hardly showed from even a middle distance, and by the fact that she spent more and more time resting in what he thought of as her nest. Shyly, rather like a lover leaving flowers at a sweetheart's doorstep, he began to bring her both a share of the cows' hay and such new grass as had begun to emerge after the rains. He left water for her as well, but she drank very little of that, seeming to take moisture—as in the old fairytales—more from the morning dew that collected on the grass and in the cups of certain leaves. Beyond that, he had no notion of what she might actually need of him, nor of how he could tell and what he could do if she were in serious discomfort.

Once or twice, when he was sitting silently by her in the night, nearly asleep, she made the little river-sound that she had made before, and he woke immediately to find her gazing at him out of eyes huge with understanding—or with sorrow for his stupidity, for all he could judge, or with bewilderment at how she could possibly have arrived at this place, this time, in her immortal life. Then he would say the only thing he knew to say to her: "Sleep, I am here," and fall back into his own wondering doze. But whether she herself actually slept or not, he could never tell.

He rarely wrote poetry during those nights when he sat lost beside the unicorn, doing nothing but listening to her breath, watching her sides move regularly in and out. But it was during one early afternoon when he had brought her a handful of the very earliest snowdrops and celandines— she would never take food from him directly, but seemed to have no objection to his watching her nibble what he set down before her—that he saw the first white ripple that was not a breath, or not her own. He did make up a poem about that; but he wrote it in his head, and by the time he got back to the house it was as vanished as any dream. He wrote another poem that night; but, as he told Giovanna Muscari, it was not nearly as good as the first. "One should never try to remake what is gone. I still forget that sometimes."

Because, as it happened, it was Giovanna, on her first day of substituting for Romano at the wheel of the blue van, who caught him tending the unicorn. Dark, slight, quick, and mischievous as her brother, but with the startlingly deep-green eyes that turned up once in every couple of Muscari generations, she had parked, as Romano always did, in front of the house, hailing him as she got down from the cab. Receiving no response, she turned and glimpsed the back of his grizzled head, his heavy shoulders bent over something she could not see.

She picked up the three computer-printed envelopes addressed to him—*two political flyers and an advertisement for something I cannot believe he would have sent away for*—and started across the field between them, calling aloud, "Signor Bianchi, here is your very own mail, personally hand-delivered at great expense, without a moment's care for her personal safety—" for Cherubino was capering along beside her, so far unthreatening, but plainly enjoying her anxiety—"by a valiant *postina* who fully expects a proper cup of coffee for her efforts . . ." The last two or three words did not emerge entirely coherently.

Bianchi leaped up with a hoarse gasp, turning to face her, as the unicorn simultaneously sprang to her feet. Giovanna, being a woman, wasted no time in denying what she saw, which was a unicorn, and—to her eye—an unquestionably pregnant one. When she found her voice, she said, mildly enough, "Actually, your mail is not very interesting. I wouldn't bother with it at all, myself."

Bianchi looked back at her without speaking, his eyes stunned and helpless beyond appeal. Giovanna said, "Someone would have found out, sooner or later. Probably my brother."

The unicorn had not fled, but had halted a little way beyond Bianchi, regarding Giovanna with a curious, wary thoughtfulness. Bianchi said accusingly, "You drive softer than he does. You sneaked up on me." But he half-laughed before he was finished, realizing the absurdity of the charge. "No, I was careless. Usually I wait until he has been and gone. But ever since . . ." He gestured, not so much toward the unicorn as toward the hollow that she had arranged to receive her newborn when the time came. "I cannot tell when it might happen—it is not like with a cow—and I need to be here. I was thinking that tonight perhaps I might sleep . . ."

"Then you would catch a cold to no purpose," Giovanna interrupted him. "I am no farmer, but I can look at her and know that she will not give birth for some weeks yet—at least three, maybe more. Men!" and she shook her head in a certain resigned annoyance that her brother would have recognized. She stepped past Bianchi, holding out her hand to the unicorn, who stayed where she was. She asked, "No one else knows?"

"No one has seen her." Bianchi smiled crookedly. "It is something to have a reputation for being a bad-tempered hermit." But his expression remained anxious.

Giovanna hooked her thumbs into her belt and leaned back on her heels, much in the manner of Romano, which it would have infuriated her to realize. "Stop looking at me like that. Of course I will tell no one—what sort of person do you think I am? But there are conditions attached."

"There would be. Are you not a Muscari?" But there was no spite or mockery in Bianchi's voice—nothing but relief. "Name these conditions, then."

"First—" Giovanna ticked the clauses off briskly on her fingers—"you will give me your telephone number, so that I can call you every evening to inquire about her health and her . . . progress. Second—"

She was interrupted by one of Bianchi's explosive snorts. "As though you could be any sort of help if she were in any sort of trouble. You know less about her than I do, and I know nothing."

Giovanna nodded, tapping a second finger on her palm. "Just so. So you and I must trust her to have this little one by herself, without getting in her way. Do not make yourself ill spending your nights out here with her; do not concern yourself with feeding her, not as long as she is on her feet. After that . . . after that, I think she will tell you what she needs. Yes, I am quite sure she will let you know."

Surprisingly, Bianchi uttered a slow, rusty chuckle. "Because you are sure that she is just like you, and you would never hesitate to let anyone know if you needed something. Very well, I agree to that. And the third condition?"

Giovanna was a long time in answering him. She looked away across the hollow at the watchful unicorn, and it seemed to Bianchi that something soundless passed between them in which he had no part. When Giovanna turned back to him, her manner was that of the small, shy, dark girl tagging silently behind her brother, clutching her stuffed monkey. She said, "Would you read me one of your poems about her?"

The request—so clearly not a condition—caught Bianchi amidships, leaving him literally wordless, though he spluttered a good deal. Even Romano, with all his sly prodding about the poetry, had never really asked to see any of it. Giovanna's voice was nearly inaudible, but her eyes met his directly, *and she doesn't do that twisting thing with her hair she used to do when she was nervous. How do I remember that?* Giovanna said, "My brother makes jokes all the time about you writing poems. When I saw her, *I* wanted to write a poem, and I have never done such a thing in my whole life. So, when I see you with her . . ."

Her voice trailed away, and she did not attempt to finish the sentence. Bianchi had no idea of what to say to her, so what came out of his mouth had no thought at all behind it. "I will tell you the first one. Maybe it is the one you wanted to write."

Giovanna frowned uncertainly. Bianchi scratched his head and closed his eyes. "Listen."

It took him a long time, not because of the poem's length, nor because he had forgotten so much as a word, but rather because having a listener disconcerted him. Giovanna's attentive eyes and the way she clasped her hands in front of her made him at times cough and stammer, or lose his place and have to start a line over. He often thought that it might still be the best poem he had yet written about the unicorn; but Giovanna's presence made him increasingly unsure of this, and he disliked the feeling greatly. Nevertheless, he repeated it all the way to the end, and then turned abruptly away, saying over his shoulder, "I have work to do. So do you."

Giovanna caught up with him within a few strides, catching hold of his coatsleeve and pulling him to face her. "Yes. Yes, that is just the way I felt when I first saw her. If I could write a poem, I would have written exactly that. Thank you. Here is your mail."

Speechless for a second time in a matter of minutes, Bianchi finally managed to grunt, "Welcome." Giovanna said nothing further, and they walked in silence to the blue mail van. As she stepped into the cab, she reminded him, "I will call tonight. Just to ask about her."

Bianchi nodded. He handed the three envelopes back to her, raising his eyebrows slightly. Giovanna said, "I will throw them away for you."

Watching the van careen away down the steep

road, he surprised and irritated himself by calling after her, "Be careful!" *The child does not have a license, I am sure of it. Who would give such a little girl a driver's license?* Yet he stood where he was for a time, until he heard the cows calling to be brought into the barn and milked. *I hope Romano has warned her about the curve near old Frascati's farm. It can be dangerous going downhill, and she drives too fast.*

Giovanna did telephone him that night, as she had said she would do. He told her shortly that there was nothing to tell her: the unicorn had not gone into labor, or anything like it, but had grazed periodically—most often in the company of Cherubino and one or two of the cats—and seemingly dozed in the hollow at times, but never for long. "I am not sure that she ever sleeps, not truly. It is all very strange, her being here. Writing the poems does not make it any less strange."

"Romano has found a book at the library. There is a lot about unicorns in it. I will read it tonight. I am to drive the mail van on Fridays, so I will see you then."

"I will look for you," Bianchi said, but she had already hung up.

In the weeks that followed, the unicorn's pregnancy became more evident—even someone who was not a farmer, like Romano, would have noticed the change—but her behavior altered not at all. She did spend more time resting in the hollow, nearly invisible in the shadow of the earthen overhang, but still capable of being up and gone in a soundless swirl of cloven hooves. Bianchi would watch her for long minutes and hours, immobile himself, and sometimes ask her aloud, "What can you be thinking? What do you remember, so graceful, so serene, gazing so far away, so far beyond my tired fields? What dreams come to you as you lie there open-eyed?" for she never closed them entirely while he was near. "Do you dream about the one who is coming—do you wonder about . . ." and he would invariably stop at that point, even in the poems. Even the poems never pursued that last question.

That urgency was left to Giovanna, who asked it early, and with increasing intensity as the days passed. "Where is the father, do you suppose? Where can he be, her mate?"

She was sitting on the ground close to the unicorn, closer than Bianchi himself was ever permitted, which always annoyed him. "Why do you ask me? What should I know about fathers?"

"Bianchi, a unicorn is not a cat, to go around mounting every female in season—if unicorns *have* seasons, the book is not clear. I am sure that her mate, her stallion, whatever you want to call him, knows, *knows*, that this child is to be born, and he is looking everywhere for her, to be there when it comes." She had rarely spoken this much in any one burst, and she literally ran out of breath and suffered a small coughing fit. Bianchi patted her back gingerly until it stopped.

"No book will tell us what we want to know, Romano's sister," he told her. "It was only a little while ago that I could not imagine that there could be such a wonder in the world as what we look on together in this moment, you and I. Perhaps her mate will come for her and the child, and perhaps not—it will all be according to the ways of unicorns."

He paused, uncomfortably aware of Giovanna's green, listening eyes. There was a small heart-shaped birthmark at the corner of the left one. "But this much I do know. This I will tell you. Seeing her even one time would have changed the poetry forever, just as it happened to Dante, who saw Beatrice only once, at a May Day party when she was eight years old. I have seen her every day now for months—a magic, an enchantment, walking around my farm, eating weeds with my goat—and it has made me different. I cannot even say how different, different in what ways—only that I am." He blinked rapidly, though Giovanna saw no tears in his eyes. He said, "When she is gone, then perhaps I will know."

When Romano asked whether she had detected any signs of a woman appearing in Claudio Bianchi's life, Giovanna would shrug with practiced disdain. "I am never in his house, what can I tell you? I do what you do—I drop off the mail and I go, *punto e basta*. As far as I can tell, he lives alone, as he has always done." Sometimes, merely for the pleasure of teasing her brother, she might add, "Of course, he might have a friend who comes to visit now and again. That does happen, you know."

Romano disapproved of the possibility. "He is an old man. He needs someone there, someone who will take care of him."

Giovanna would most often shrug again. "Perhaps so. Me, I ask him no questions. Go away, I have studying to do." Once or twice, to plague him further, she remarked lightly, "He is not quite as old as all that, you know."

Spring comes earlier in Calabria than to anywhere else in Italy. The sunrise howling of the *tramontane* winds gradually decreases, and is most often followed by the warm, wet southwesterly flow of the *sirocco* that can bring flowers out of the ground before the weather is quite ready for them. Bianchi himself often felt a childlike desire to run around warning the new poppies and blossoming bergamot trees, "Not yet, not so soon, it is a trick! The cold rains will return and beat you back into the earth—stay down, stay down a while longer!" But this year there seemed no danger of such a betrayal: the days warmed steadily, the soft young grass was welcomed eagerly by cows grown weary of stale hay, the three cats roamed more widely, and even Garibaldi stayed outside on some nights without whining to be let in. Bianchi saw black storks going over, and heard the cries of northbound geese in the night.

The unicorn grew heavier and somewhat slower afoot, eating little, but drowsing often in the returning sun. The life within her was visibly more active, most often in the afternoon, and Giovanna made a point of timing her Friday mail deliveries accordingly. She never offered to take Romano's route more than one day a week. "Because he will become suspicious, immediately. He is not nearly as stupid as he acts."

Bianchi looked puzzled. Giovanna felt oddly embarrassed, and annoyed with herself for feeling so. "He will think I have a lover."

"Oh," Bianchi said. "Well, you don't." After a moment he added, "Do you?"

Giovanna raised one black eyebrow before she answered. "No fear. They are all too much like Romano around here, nervous if you roam too far away from the stove and the bed. I certainly hope his Tessa can cook for him when I graduate and run off with his mail van."

Bianchi said nothing, not always being entirely certain when Giovanna was joking. They were standing together, watching the unicorn grazing alone in his vineyard, where he had first seen her. Neither spoke for some while—Giovanna was proving an almost distressingly comfortable person to be silent with—until she finally said, "It will be soon. The new one wants to be born." She never referred to the coming infant in any other way.

"It will happen in the middle of the night," Bianchi grumbled. "It always happens so with the pigs, always."

"Bianchi, a unicorn is not a pig, any more than she is a cat. It will happen, I think, when she decides that it is time." After a long, thoughtful moment, she added, "Perhaps it *has* to be born on your farm, for some reason we will never know. *Chi lo sa?* Perhaps she came from some other century, all the way across the ages, just so her child could take its first breath right here."

She tugged at her hair, something she did only in moments of anxiety. "What troubles me is that I will not be here for the birth. Unless it is on a Friday."

Bianchi was silent for a long time before he surprised himself by blurting out, "Then I hope it does happen on a Friday." Giovanna turned her head to look at him. He said, "I would feel . . . better if you were here."

After some while, Giovanna said, "Yes."

They went on staring straight ahead, watching the unicorn nibbling on fallen grape leaves. Bianchi said presently, "I call her *La Signora* sometimes. Not for her to answer to, but just for me, inside." Giovanna nodded without answering.

———

The birth did not come on a Friday, but on a Thursday, and it came on such a night of wind and rain as had not been seen for a month. The *sirocco* has no specific season, but blows as and where it chooses, at times almost as fiercely as the *tramontane*. Yet it was not the wind that awakened Bianchi, but Cherubino on his hind legs, butting at the bedroom's single window with nose and horns. One look at the goat's demonic, desperate face, and Bianchi was out of the house, barefoot, a raincoat thrown over his old-fashioned flannel nightshirt, stumbling toward the hollow where the unicorn lay on her side. Her eyes were open and clear, and she was breathing calmly, but Cherubino knew, and so did Bianchi. Without thinking, he crouched beside her—far closer than he had ever dared approach— and put his hand on her neck where it joined her body. He felt the immortal heartbeat against his palm, and for a moment he shut his eyes. He moved his hand to her belly and listened.

"The child is coming the wrong way, *Signora*," he said, raising his voice against the wind. "I know what to do, but you will have to trust that I know." The unicorn lay still under his hands. "Well, then. So." *Salt, soft against my eyes . . . the Doctor's Wind, blowing home from the sea—that must surely be a good sign, surely . . .*

The rain began as he was trying to find a courteous manner to keep the unicorn's tail out of the way. She lay half-sheltered by the overhang of the hollow, with most of her body exposed to the increasing downpour. Bianchi grunted with distant annoyance, pulling off the ancient raincoat to throw over her. He held up his hands to the pounding rain—at least they would be as clean as possible—and went on talking to the unicorn, telling her and himself, "It will go well, we will go well, do not be afraid . . ." *I must not let her be afraid—her or the little one.* "It will go well, *Signora*—my beauty, my sweetheart . . ."

It did not go well, not in the beginning. The colt—as he had finally determined to think of it—was almost impossible to turn, and Bianchi could feel its terror all along his arm, no matter how comfortingly he spoke to it. Throwing all his strength into the effort, *if I can get hold of that foreleg, the one folded up so tightly, but what if it breaks?* he pushed blindly *but what if it breaks? what if the little one is strangling in the cord right now just the way don't think about it the same way don't ever think about it* . . . Then suddenly the small body began to come almost too easily, so that he was first alarmed at the possibility of the sharp tiny hooves hurting the mother—though *La Signora* remained as placid as he could have wished—and then of the colt having died before it had ever lived. *O God, God, what will I do then, what will I say?* Yet he kept sensing its living fear in his own body, *that has to be a good sign*, and tried to imagine what it would be like to see Giovanna running to the hollow in the morning.

Then a surge—a rush of watery blood—and the little head was free: damp, wild-eyed, gasping its first breath in the rain. The unicorn raised her own head, twisting her neck for a first sight of the newborn, but Bianchi said sharply, "*Aspetta, Signora*—wait, wait, lie still!" To his amazement— not then, but afterward—the unicorn obeyed, as he bit the cord in the oldest of ways, and slowly guided her child, slick and wriggly as a tadpole, into the screaming world, trying to shield it from the storm with his body. *The horn is just a tiny bud, of course, it would hurt her otherwise.* In a vague way, he noticed that the newborn's coat shone as black, even through the rain, as its mother's shone white. *Like her hair . . .*

When he brought the baby's mouth to a distended nipple, the unicorn made the river-sound that he had heard before, so softly that he barely heard it under the wind. Soaked and frozen himself, strengthless, he huddled as close to her as her child did, and it seemed to him then that she provided sheltering warmth for the three of them. It seemed also that he heard, in his exhausted sleep, the weeping of the black-haired woman *like broken glass in my heart her tears,* and he buried his face against the unicorn's belly until he could not hear the weeping anymore.

That was how Giovanna found them when she managed at last to coax and command the blue van up the hill road, spongy with rain and doubly treacherous even with the storm blown over and the sun shining. The black newborn was already trying to stand on shaky legs too long to manage, but the unicorn lay as patiently still as ever while Bianchi slept like the dead across her body. Indeed, Giovanna thought, for one heart-numbing moment, that he really might be dead, so motionless he lay. She had to kneel close before she heard him snoring gently; if she thanked God, she was quiet about it. One moment to disbelieve the wonder of a unicorn's breath in her palm; then she was hauling Bianchi to his bare, muddy feet, tugging his arm across her shoulder, coaxing him. "*Vieni . . . vieni, amico . . .* come on, come on, my friend. Time to go home . . ."

Lurching the first few steps with him, she almost stumbled into what she took at first for a shallow depression, and then realized as a hoofprint, cloven as precisely as *La Signora's*, but distinctly deeper and broader than those. When she turned her head, she could see them circling the hollow until they vanished—whether among a stand of olive trees or into the bright new sky, she could not tell, and there was no time to study them further.

Somehow she half-dragged Bianchi all the way back to his house, pulled his nightshirt off over his head, rubbed him dry unashamedly—Romano was not her only brother—then wrestled him into his bed, and poured coffee, liberally infused with *grappa*, into him until he coughed and waved it away. With his eyes closed, he said, "It was turned around . . . the little one . . . it did not know the way." His voice was hoarse and slow. "I tried so hard . . . I am sorry . . ."

Giovanna stared at him. Bianchi put his hands over his face. He whispered a name that she did not catch. "I am sorry . . . I am so sorry . . ."

"Bianchi, they are both well," Giovanna said. "The little one is almost standing. Do you hear me, Bianchi?" He did not answer her. She said, "Sleep. She can take care of it now."

At the door, without turning, she said, "I was afraid for you." She left without hearing Bianchi's reply, which he missed himself, being asleep at the time.

". . . wished you there."

He slept late into the afternoon. On waking, he dressed himself, drank a great deal of water, and foraged absently in the refrigerator for a few remains of last evening's dinner. He let the cows out, and then walked slowly to the hollow, accompanied by Cherubino and all three of the cats. The unicorns—mother and son, white and black—appeared to be waiting for him there, the colt notably firmer on its legs than he would have expected, *La Signora* as calmly elegant as though Bianchi had never had an entire hairy arm inside her, groping blindly in her darkness for her child.

For a moment she put her head lightly on Bianchi's shoulder, and, as he had never done, he touched the horn. It felt smooth and harsh to his fingers at the same time: there were hard, slightly raised rings at regular intervals under the sleek spiral surface, ascending to the tip, as far as he could judge, having no mind to chance the gleaming tip. La Signora *is a dangerous animal.* La Signora *is very dangerous.*

"You must be careful," he said to her. "You did well to choose this place when you knew *he* was coming, because so few people ever visit me, and your folk know everything about living unseen. But *he* changes things." Bianchi could not tell whether or not the colt understood him as *La Signora* did, but the little one was watching him just as intently, out of the same deeply dark eyes. Simply by the way in which he braced his new legs, standing beside his mother, Bianchi would have known him for a male of any species.

"He changes things. You will not be able to travel until he can keep up with you, and meanwhile you are more visible together, even here. Children are—" he hesitated painfully, *what can I know about children? I only know kittens, calves, poems—* "children are curious, *Signora*, children want to go and see. You must make him understand . . ."

Here he stopped, this time for good, because the ludicrousness of admonishing an immortal creature to be careful was a little more than his sense of the absurd could tolerate. He reached out a hand to the colt, which promptly skittered away from him, as though they had not been intimately involved mere hours before; the gesture ended awkwardly on the cheek of *La Signora*. She regarded him out of a dark kindness that made his eyes ache, and he was the one who stepped back and lowered his gaze. "I will keep you safe. You and him."

He had not been back in the house for ten minutes before Giovanna called him. She was crying.

"Forgive me . . . I didn't *mean* . . ." It took Bianchi a few moments to recognize the nearly hysterical voice as hers, and longer to comprehend what she was telling him. "I didn't mean to . . . but seeing her, seeing her and the little one, I came home on wings, on *wings*, and Romano . . . Romano took one look at me and he *saw*, and he *asked*, and he kept on, he kept asking . . . and I was, I was so happy, and so . . . *forgive* me, Claudio . . ."

He was too bewildered, and increasingly alarmed, to take in the fact that she had called him by his name for the first time. "I didn't mean, it was just . . . I was so *happy* . . ."

"What?" he demanded. "Stop crying! What are you saying?" But he already knew.

"I told him!" Giovanna wailed. "It just came out—your *Signora* and her baby . . . everything, *everything*. And he will be driving up to see them the first thing tomorrow, even though it is not a mail day. I feel like dying—I am so ashamed . . ."

"*Basta!* Stop that bawling, woman!" He shouted it the second time, as harshly as he could, and was rewarded with startled silence, punctuated by sniffles. More quietly, he said, "It is my fault as much as yours. More—if I had been paying attention the first time you came, you would never have seen her, never known. Stop blubbering now, you are not someone who *blubbers*." This provoked a startled, slightly hysterical giggle, equally as disquieting to Bianchi as her tears. "Listen to me. What happens now will be by her choice—in the end everything is by her choice, always has been. If she does not want Romano to see her—see them—then he will not see her, that is all there is to it. Wash your face and have your dinner, and go to bed. *Buona notte.*"

He was about to hang up the phone when she asked shakily, "And if she chooses to be seen? What then?"

"It has happened before. How else would we know there are such things, if no one ever saw them? Go to bed."

He wrote part of a poem that night: not about *La Signora* and her child, but about Giovanna's grief at the thought of her uncontrollable joy having betrayed the unicorn's presence. It was a new sort of poem for him, and slow in coming, and he dozed off at his kitchen table, waking only at the sound of the blue mail van chugging up the road. As he had ordered Giovanna to do, he splashed water on his face, ran a hand over his sleep-bristled hair, and went outside to meet Romano.

The sun was just up, glittering off the leaves of the beech tree a little way from the house, where the unicorn was standing, letting her child nurse. The black colt looked up when the van heaved itself around the last bend, but his mother paid no heed, even when Romano jumped down from the cab, and immediately had to scramble back up, having forgotten to set the handbrake. He did not take so much as a step toward the unicorn, nor toward Bianchi, but stood rigid, gaping, until, for all his own anxiety, it was impossible for Bianchi not to be amused. He said, "Well, I do not think I looked quite *that* stupid when I first saw her—but maybe I did. It is hard to know, of course."

Romano's eyes were almost as wild as those of a strange colt struggling through a storm to be born. He whispered, "Giovanna . . . don't be angry at her—she tried to stop me. But I had to *see* . . ."

"Well," Bianchi said. "Now you have seen. Close your mouth."

La Signora raised her head, looking directly at Romano. The dawn light turned the dark-gold horn to a fiery flower, and Romano backed a little toward the van. He said, "I'll bet she could be over here in half a second."

Bianchi nodded. Romano said with some earnestness, "Tell her I do not want to hurt her, or the little one. Tell her I just wanted to look."

"She knows that. Otherwise she would be somewhere else in half a second. I am afraid for her, not for you."

Romano looked puzzled for a moment; then his eyes widened, and he touched his fingers, first to his lips and then to his heart. "Never! What do you think I am? I would never tell *anyone*!" Bianchi looked at him. "I would *not*! I swear on my parents' graves! Giovanna will swear, too."

"Giovanna has already told," Bianchi said. "No, she did not mean to, and it was only you she told. And you will not mean to tell, either, but it will happen." He waved Romano's protests to silence. "No, it will. And there will be nothing you or your sister or I can do about it. The only real question is what *she* will decide to do, when the reporters' big vans are up here day and night, and the helicopters are hovering overhead like *avvoltoi neri*, black vultures. There will be police, too, and government people, maybe Americans wanting to make movies about her." He chuckled slowly and dryly. "*Paparazzi* chasing a unicorn all around my farm. If she allows it. *Chi lo sa?*"

La Signora, who had bent to her nursling, raised her head again, looking now toward Bianchi. *Did she hear my promise to keep her and her son safe? What can that possibly mean to her, who is about to be hunted more mercilessly by cameras than she can ever have been by mounted knights? Can even she know what is coming for her? I wish I believed in God right now, so I could ask him to have mercy on her.*

Romano left after a while, swearing over and over that he would never mention the unicorn's existence: not to his friends, no matter how drunk he might get, nor to Tessa Moro, his fiancée, no matter how much he wanted to share his wonder with her. "And, please, you must forgive Giovanna. She will never stop crying until you do, and it is giving me a headache. And breaking my heart."

"I was never angry at her. Tell her to come back. The little one is already trying to run."

But he was angry—angry and frightened by the realization of his own helplessness in the face of the twenty-first century that would inevitably be invading the life he had built for himself—*no, the life that I have settled for*—here with the trees and the animals and the earth, all granting him enough to get by on, all supporting the profitless poems that made him happy to think about, even as the farm people still called "the Greek's place" crumbled silently away through his own old disinterest.

His little television set received a couple of the stronger RAI channels, and Romano sometimes brought him day-old copies of *La Stampa* or the *Corriere della Sera*. He knew, as coldly as he knew that Giorgio Malatesta would be selling off-brand Albanian transmissions to the day he died, that when the news that he had two unicorns living on his farm got out—and it would, no matter what Romano swore, because such news wants to get out, will get out, just as *La Signora's* black colt had willed so indomitably to be born—then the world he knew would end, and end for good. Whatever happened from now on, there would be no going back to his dear now.

All of which would be tolerable—he would *make* it tolerable—if only he could keep his word to a unicorn.

Giovanna did come back, not on that day, but on the next, her usual Friday. She hesitated before she stepped down from the cab, and the hesitation was in her eyes as well as her body. It moved Bianchi in a way that was still surprising and distantly alarming to him, even as he was walking to her and putting his arms clumsily around her.

She rested her head against his head—they were very nearly of a height—and she did cry then, but only a little, and without a sound. They stood so for some time.

"*Troppo vecchio*," Bianchi said presently. "I am far too old for you." Giovanna nodded against him. "And I was living alone before you were born, and I do not really like very many people." He stroked her hair. "I like you."

"I like you, too," Giovanna whispered. "I am so sorry—"

Bianchi put a finger across her lips without answering, and they went on watching the unicorns. Giovanna said, "I think his horn is a little bigger, don't you?"

"They need to be ready," Bianchi said.

He had already seen the larger footprints before she pointed them out to him. "No, the cows never come this close to the house—they are all afraid of the goat, which makes him very vain. And the tracks are not his, either, nor hers." His eyebrows and shoulders mimicked the quirk of his mouth as he smiled at her. "You are the one who kept asking about the father, *non e vero?*"

Romano swore that he had never said anything to anyone, and Bianchi rather believed him. He thought himself that it had probably started with the Reggio traffic helicopter, which usually passed high over his farm at around three o'clock every afternoon. In any case, whatever the cause, the first result was a visit from a battered yellow two-door Fiat, whose transmission sounded no better than the Studebaker's. The Fiat contained two raincoated reporters, not from Reggio, as Bianchi would have expected, but from Siderno Marina, farther up the coast. They were coy about stating their mission, asking diffidently about rumors, local folktales, sightings—even mentioning mermaids reported playing in the Strait of Messina, and *la leggenda Americana* Bigfoot—and Bianchi found it easy to play the slack-jawed peasant, since they expected one. They went away without bothering to stroll around the farm, or even to check the earth under their feet for the prints of delicate cloven hooves. *Well, if they're all to be as blind-stupid as that pair . . .* But he was a Calabrese, and knew better than to expect such fortune.

That night, he did something that he never told Giovanna about. When he judged it late enough that the village streets would be comparatively empty, he started the Studebaker—not the easiest chore on his farm—and drove slowly down into town, coaxing and cursing the truck in a soft undertone all the way. He left it on a dark back street and walked on to the one-room cottage, little bigger than a chicken coop, that served as the reception area, workplace, and residence of Madame Leonora Venucci.

The door opened before he reached it. This did not particularly startle Bianchi; it was known in the village that Madame Leonora (as she preferred to be addressed, in the French style) possessed a familiar spirit who always informed her when clients—or children bent on mischief—were approaching her dark doorstep. Bianchi himself most often believed that the old woman merely had extremely acute hearing, as well as a number of loose paving stones in the pathway to her house. This generally informed his attitude toward *la strega*: he held no special belief in her powers, but there had been moments over the years when he wondered . . . and anyway, what could it hurt? Now he said simply, "Good evening, Madame."

"I knew you would come to me tonight," the tiny old woman wheezed. "I knew when you made up your mind to come."

Despite the lateness of the hour, Madame Leonora was still in her working clothes, which consisted of a green turban, a once-purple robe long washed to a pallid violet, more or less matching opera gloves, and brown house slippers the size of small dogs. No one could remember her ever wearing anything else—except, when she deemed her visitor important enough to warrant it, a floor-length midnight-blue fur cloak with a high flaring collar, and a certain vaguely disconcerting smell. Bianchi knew it only by reputation.

"I knew you would come," the old woman said again. "Madame Leonora always knows." Bianchi grunted in response, looked quickly around, and followed her into the house.

To do Madame Leonora justice, the single room, lighted by a single tottery lamp, was remarkably neat and well-kept. The spangled cloth on the small round table was frowsy with age, but quite clean, and there was no evidence either of a crystal ball, a wand, a yellowing skull, or even a deck of tarot cards. To left and right tall wardrobes guarded their secrets; under one of the pair of high-backed chairs, a one-eyed cat, properly black, hissed sullenly at Bianchi. The several vases on the deep window ledge were elegant enough to belong in a very different house, but the flowers they contained badly needed to be replaced. Books with crumbling leather bindings were ranged on a shelf beside the little wood stove, and—surprisingly—a framed portrait of the Virgin held the place of honor in a niche directly above the door. There was a fire in the stove, and the house was warm.

"Sit," said Madame Leonora, and Bianchi took

his cap off and sat. The old woman took the chair across the table from him and glared at him out of small currant-colored eyes. "Well, you certainly took your time about it," she grumbled presently. "You have taken so long that I am doubtful whether I can help you at all. But then you were always a stubborn mocker, always, since you were a small boy."

"You never knew me when I was small," Bianchi reminded her. "You came here from Lucca when I was practically grown."

Taken aback, Madame Leonora frowned under brows so pale, and so fiercely plucked, as to be almost invisible. "*Ay*, that was the other boy," she muttered to herself, slapping her cheek lightly. "Well, you will grow old too, Bianchi. Now, about the Muscari girl—"

"I am not here because of her," Bianchi interrupted, raising his voice more than he had meant to. He was only mildly startled that *la strega* was aware of his relationship with Giovanna: having lived most of his life in or near small southern villages, he would have been far more surprised if she had not. It was Madame Leonora's business, and that of every such rural practitioner, to know very nearly as much about her neighbors as she pretended to know. Even so, Giovanna's name, in the fortune-teller's harsh rasp, made him flush sharply, and angered him. He said, "Nothing to do with her. Nothing."

"Of course not," the old woman agreed quickly. "Madame Leonora always knows. You are concerned about that shortness of breath you have been experiencing late at night—" Bianchi looked back at her without responding. *Why on earth did I ever imagine a silly, half-mad old fraud could help me?* Madame Leonora corrected herself again. "No, *permesso*, I again confuse you with someone else, *scusami*. This is a matter of animals, not so?"

Bianchi waited, annoyed to realize that he was holding his breath. "I mean, the strange plague of udder abscesses spreading among your sows. Madame Leonora long ago created her own special remedy for this tragic ailment." Bianchi chuckled dryly, and the witch bridled. "Ah, you laugh? Shall I tell you what became of the last lout of a pig farmer foolish enough to laugh at Madame Leonora Venucci?" She appeared to consider relating the cautionary tale, then rejected the notion. "No, I was too cruel on that occasion, and I still rather regret it. I should never have cursed *all* his pigs—just the sows. But I was younger then."

"I have six weanling pigs," Bianchi replied. "And one sow."

"Did I say *pigs?*" Madame Leonora blinked, inserting a finger under the turban to scratch her head. "*Ay,* this thing of age—I cannot even talk properly anymore. Of course I was speaking of your cows, the poor things. If you had delayed any further in coming to me . . ."

Bianchi stood up while she was saying, "Your cabbages are suffering from the Tunisian Black Pestilence—this is why they are coming up so pale and scanty. And *somebody* has also put a curse on your onions . . ."

"*Buona notte,* Madame Leonora," Bianchi said. He put his cap back on and went to the door, hunching his shoulders slightly against the fusillade of good, round, filthy Calabrese curses that were bound to pursue him. But she said nothing further until he was standing once again on her doorstep, shaking his head in continuing anger at himself, still smelling the curious, almost-familiar herbs that smoldered in her fireplace. *I hope the transmission will not fall out until I am home. It will be uphill.*

Behind him, the wheezing voice, no more than a crackle, a rustle. "Bianchi." He did not answer. "Bianchi. Your wife did not leave you because the baby died." There was a silence for a little, which was good, because Bianchi could not have comprehended language in that moment. Then: "She left because you did."

The light in the single room went out. Madame Leonora's work was done for the day.

The Studebaker stalled three times on the crawl home.

The next film crew—three this time—was indeed from Reggio Calabria, and they came in a better car, with a television camera. These were brisk as police, though plainly slightly embarrassed to be asking questions about unicorns being reported on his property. And they not only noticed the betraying hoofprints, but filmed them; and at least one was country enough not to be fobbed off with talk of cows and calves. In neither instance were *La Signora* and her little son anywhere to be seen, but Bianchi had no faith that this would remain the case. It was a small farm, after all, and they shone so.

As well as he imagined himself decently prepared for all the vans and RVs and video trucks that came scrambling up the road, there was no way Bianchi could have conceived of what it would mean to have the twenty-first century crash into his near-nineteenth-century life like a runaway truck. He was endlessly interviewed blinking into more television lenses than he could keep track of, growling at each blonde young lady or trim young man holding a microphone that he had no idea how the *porca miseria* story ever got started. Unicorns were just as mythical as mermaids, even children knew that today, and these *porca miseria* motorcycles and cameras were frightening his animals and keeping him from running his farm, and he had no more than that to say. That was all any of them got out of him, and sooner or later they would all turn their machines off, turn their vans around, and go away, blaming one another for the waste of time.

He had rather hoped—foolishly, as it quickly turned out—that the comparative remoteness of his farm, combined with boredom and frustration at their unwelcoming reception, might provide something of a bulwark against the cars and the cameras. But the news helicopters were another matter. Bianchi had expected them, as he had warned Romano to expect them, as he expected the Reggio weather helicopter every day, and now and then a police spotter, flying low in search of a terrorist or a lost child. Now, however, there were few days when he did not waken to the sound of engines outside his door, or fall asleep with bright lights still stabbing into his window. Even so, he clung doggedly to his belief in the innate impatience of everyone who was not a farmer. "I tell them nothing," he said to Giovanna on the phone, "and there is nothing for them to see or to show, so what can they do? It will all pass. In time they will get tired. People get tired of everything."

"I hope so," Giovanna said doubtfully; but Romano, delivering the mail, said, "Not of unicorns.

They are the ultimate tourist attraction. I was wrong about the skiers and the beach people."

"It will all pass," Bianchi repeated. His eyes were dark and distant, and the lines down his cheeks were more pronounced than Romano had ever seen them. He mentioned this to his sister.

But the rumors seemed to spread upward in one grand synchronized flurry, like a flock of birds all taking flight in a single rush, wheeling as one in the same direction, crying the same cry. Within two weeks, the helicopters crowding each other in the sky now bore the emblems of radio and television stations he had never heard of—a good half of them, and more every day, from other countries, and even other continents. He was interviewed in languages he did not know, translated to the world by people who did not speak Calabrese—and, in some cases, barely spoke Italian.

Nor did these helicopters fly off to their nests with the coming of evening: on the contrary, many of them hovered all night, sweeping the entire countryside with powerful searchlights that crisscrossed each other like whiplashes, invariably waking him and setting Garibaldi barking and cowering under the house. Then Bianchi would pull the bedclothes over his head, and do his best to drown out the engine racket with his own cursing.

Romano, bringing him the newest package of quite touching gifts from children for the baby unicorn, said, "Alas, my friend, you are news, and there is no getting away from news. It would be like getting away from yourself."

"There is nothing in the world that I would like more," Bianchi sighed, closing his eyes at the sound of motorcycles nearby. The lighter Aprilias and Cagivas appeared to be the vehicles of choice for very young men hunting unicorns across his land. Complaints to *Tenente* Esposito brought a helpless shrug and a scattering of warning notices tacked to random trees, which were either ignored or vandalized. "Bianchi, half your trespassers are my men. I can warn them, I can discharge them—but if I do that, I won't have enough police left to patrol a church football match, a village dance. *Pazienzia*, Bianchi. Ignore them, that's what I would do— just ignore them. You wouldn't have any more of that Amarone left?"

Even old—very old—Aldo Frascati told Bianchi, "They have this thing now, my granddaughter showed me. It is on the computer, you can find anybody anywhere in the world. My granddaughter, she hits this key, that key, and there is my house—*my house*—right there on the screen. I asked her, can the computer come inside and show me sitting on the *gabinetto*, and she said no, she doesn't think so. Not yet."

It was just after Bianchi learned about Google Earth that the animal-rights people showed up on his doorstep. They arrived in a large and very vocal group, equipped with signs and bullhorns, through which they informed Bianchi that they had been monitoring his treatment of God's most beautiful and mystical creatures, and that they had complaints. They also had lawyers, which gave them more headlines than the various groups who regarded the unicorn either as an incarnation of the Virgin, or the first appearance in centuries of the *chi-lin*, magical and revered. Catholics or Confucians, this latter group came to worship, not to sue, but they kept building shrines all over Bianchi's farm, for him to destroy and themselves to rebuild. And they were by far the hardest to get rid of.

Bianchi stopped answering the telephone, even for the chance of a call from Giovanna. The interview requests continued unabated, but he turned even more monosyllabic than before, and the newsmen quickly became as bored as he had foretold, and began interviewing one another, and the unicorn hunters, and any neighbors they could find, no matter how distant. For most of them— even the veterans, who generally regarded the whole affair as a local publicity fraud—it was the biggest story of their careers, and they were not about to let it get away.

On Fridays, when Giovanna appeared in the blue van, the reporters would swoop down on her in a pure feeding frenzy, hoping frantically that she might turn out to be other than a mere postmistress—Bianchi's lover, surely, or perhaps some young virgin come to capture the unicorn in the traditional manner. For her own amusement, at such moments, she tended to speak incomprehensibly in a loose, thick mountain-Swiss accent, appearing plainly incapable even of spelling the name of the creature everyone was asking her about. Bianchi was terse with her then, not wanting to give anyone any further reason to press her for information. She would hand him his mail, then wink at him, and be gone again in a matter of minutes. But the one wink usually made the chaos that had come upon him very nearly bearable.

But there was no retreating to the poems, as he had done in other bad times; they withheld themselves, as everything in his life seemed to be doing at present. Cherubino, plainly pining after *La Signora*, began to look his age; and Garibaldi, frightened by the continuing chaos, hid under the house more and more. The cows were in a similar state, reluctant to leave their barn at all, and nervous enough when they did that they produced far less milk than usual. One of them—Gianetta, it was, normally the most tractable of the three— turned on a particularly annoying motorcyclist and chased him so fiercely on his little Honda that he spilled the bike into a blackberry bush, to much applause from his competitors. The other hunters afforded the cows a somewhat wider berth after that.

On the very rare occasions when Bianchi found himself actually alone on his farm—*no wonder the poems won't come, how did I ever take it so for granted, my lovely solitude?*—La Signora would even more rarely appear, followed both by her son, already a third the size of a grown male, and a certain contentment, inexplicable but profound, that almost compensated, but not quite, for the loss of his poetry. He was happy to see her, but in a quieter way than he had ever been.

"Why are you here, *Signora?*" he asked the unearthly glory under his apple trees one unseasonably soft night. The unicorn looked up at his voice, while her son continued nibbling on windfalls, half-mouthing, half-playing with them. Her eyes, as always, reached through Bianchi's own and beyond them, to the farthest recesses of his heart. The Virgin's eyes were supposed to do that to you, but Bianchi had never found it so, even as a child. "Why are you here? Yes, you were waiting to welcome *him*, even a stupid farmer understands that in time . . . but why do you stay on my little scratch of ground, when you can fly across the wide world as you choose, when wiser hunters than these louts here, and far better poets than I, will all rise alike to worship you and try to kill you? What can you be waiting for now?"

White-gold as a northern sunrise, she made no response to his questions, but stayed near him all that night, while the black unicorn frisked about the apple orchard in the moonlight, sometimes rearing comically on his slender back legs, as unicorns are so often depicted, and so rarely do. Bianchi eventually fell asleep with his back uncomfortably against a tree; when he woke, stiff and lonely, both unicorns were gone, off to turn invisible in some deep wrinkle of his acreage, though he could never fathom how they managed never to be flushed from cover by a phalanx of yearning yokels. *Do you know, do you ever consider, how beautiful and impossible you have made my life? Do you care?*

He saw the other, deeper hoofprints three times, once so near his house that he was surprised to have heard nothing about it from Garibaldi or Cherubino. On the other two occasions, he had been patrolling the scrubby hills at the untended edges of his property: something he did when he could spare the time, in vague hopes of warning off vagrant unicorn hunters. In both cases he erased the tracks as carefully as he could, and went home looking over his shoulder, feeling like a trespasser himself on his own land. He never mentioned them to Giovanna, though he could not have said why.

One afternoon in what felt like early spring but was more properly late winter, while he was replacing a fan belt on his tractor, he was approached by a monster. The monster was middle-aged, and wore a tan topcoat in approved movie style, slung around his wide shoulders. He was notably better dressed than almost all of the unicorn hunters, whether they arrived by helicopter or laboring Vespa: they had come clad for utility, after all, and they might have mocked him for being a toff or a dandy . . . but they knew him, and they kept their distance.

The monster sauntered up beside Bianchi, who was too occupied to notice him at first, and peered into the exposed engine with a knowledgeably scornful air. "Bertolini, hey? Underpowered, even for a handkerchief-sized place like yours. Hard to get parts, too."

Bianchi turned to study the monster slowly and thoughtfully. The monster was actually shorter than he was, with the deep chest and flaring nose of an opera singer; he carried himself with the subdued swagger of a much taller man, with nothing to prove. He gave his name, which Bianchi did not recognize, but he knew a monster when he saw one.

"'*Ndrangheta*, is it?" he asked politely. "I wondered how long it would be."

The monster smiled. He had large, strong-looking teeth, showing almost no stains, despite the Cigarro Toscano jutting up between them. *That American actor, in the cowboy movies—he smoked Toscanos. I remember.* "I am pleased that you did not confuse us with the Mafia. So many do."

"What do you want?" Bianchi asked. "I have work to do."

"Of course you do," the monster agreed. "But this should not take long. How much for the unicorns?"

"The unicorns do not belong to me." Bianchi's hands were slipping on the new fan belt, but he kept his voice down to a casual grunt, and did not look at the monster. "You are an intelligent man, you must know that."

"*Mmm.*" The monster nodded. "How much, then, for a farm with a couple of unicorns on it?"

"That would be a foolish offer from an intelligent man. Unicorns go where they please. You must know that too."

The monster crowded gracefully past Bianchi to crane farther under the old tractor's hood. He brushed the long ash from his cigar tip with a tap of his little finger, and it in turn brushed Bianchi's hand as it fell into the engine. "*Impacciato, goffo!*" he berated himself. "My apologies, I am so clumsy. I should not be around machines—things just seem to *happen*. You know how it is with some people."

"It is nothing." Bianchi was consciously taking long, slow breaths as he worked, trying to slow down his racketing pulse.

"On the contrary," the monster replied. "It is not nothing at all." He flicked the cigar again, and more ash fell.

Bianchi took a last deep breath and turned to face the monster directly. The monster's eyes were brown and friendly, with deep space beyond them. Bianchi said, "I will only tell you this once, because you already know what I am going to say. Nothing here is for sale. Not because you are who you are, but because I do not choose to sell my home to anyone, especially a *pezzo di merda* like you. I like it here."

"Ah." The monster seemed to take no offense at all. He nodded again. "Well, if you should ever decide that you like it here a bit less, you might let me know." And he produced from his vest pocket, tucked neatly behind the Toscanos, an ivory-white card with his name on it in raised letters. "I will not trouble you further. Unless you call the number on that card, you will not be hearing from me again. *Buon giorno*, Mr. Bianchi."

A Japanese helicopter was circling overhead as the monster walked away, and he waved to it without turning his head. A jeep with what looked like a harpoon gun mounted on the hood, followed too closely by a television van from a Messina station, started to cut across the monster's path until the jeep driver—clad in camouflage clothing, like many of the hunters—recognized him and hit the brakes so hard that the jeep went up on its rear wheels, and the van smacked into it, jolting it into a half-spin, and producing a volley of screams, curses, and the distinct sound of buckling metal. The monster walked calmly by.

Bianchi leaned against the tractor, waiting for the trembling that had spread from his heart to his entire freezing body to die down. *'Ndrangheta . . . I said "a piece of shit like you" to the 'Ndrangheta. And he most courteously told me that I'd live to beg him to take my farm. I am insane. I am an insane imbecile. I am dead.*

When his hands were steady enough for the work, he fitted and adjusted the fan belt, closed the tractor hood, then walked straight back to his house, and—perhaps the strangest thing he ever did in his entire life—sat down at the kitchen table and wrote a poem. The telephone rang three times, and reporters knocked twice at his door, but Bianchi hardly noticed. He worked on his poem for the rest of the afternoon; and when he decided it was finished, he drank two glasses of the Melissa Gaglioppo and telephoned Giovanna Muscari. *Like a schoolboy, like a schoolboy with pimples and a high, piping voice. Your life is running backward, Bianchi.*

He did not tell her about the encounter with the monster. He said simply, "I have missed you."

"I, too." Giovanna spoke so low that he knew Romano must be nearby. "There is too much confusion, there are too many people, watching everything. I did not want to make it all harder for you."

"I miss you," Bianchi said again. "I miss your voice. I am still too old, and too mean, and it is breaking my throat to say this, but I have missed you very badly."

Giovanna did not answer immediately, but there was a smile in her voice when she did. "You are not mean. Cranky is different."

Bianchi laughed then, for what seemed the first time in years, or in his life. "Well, that is a great compliment. I thank you."

"I will come as soon as I can," Giovanna said. "Before Friday. I will make Romano lend me his motorcycle."

Bianchi was astonished. "Can you drive a motorcycle, too? What a wonder."

"I am sure I can—do not worry." Giovanna hung up. Bianchi bit his lip, *of course, everybody can drive a motorcycle, everybody except you,* and went outside to attend to the pigs.

The two young men with the harpoon-jeep were still working on the stove-in back end into the early evening. Bianchi lent them a couple of wrenches, made a suggestion or two, and asked them, "Why are you hoping to kill the unicorns? Why would you not just take pictures, videos, with your cell phones, your fancy digital cameras, and let them be?"

The young men looked at him, and then at each other, in plain astonishment. They were not bad or vicious young men—Bianchi even knew the father of one of them, who was a doctor in Reggio. They replied by turns, but they might as well have been speaking in unison. "What would be the point of that? Without the horn, the skull, all mounted on the wall, what would it *mean*?" Bianchi said nothing more, but helped them make the jeep drivable—at least, to take them home—and stood looking after them for some time when they left.

Matteo Falcone, who had never before been to his house, came to visit the next morning, while Bianchi was repairing the damage caused by a reporter's car to his onion field. Bianchi disliked Falcone as seriously as he bothered to dislike anyone, regarding him as a gangster little better than the *'Ndrangheta*, taking advantage of his neighbors, who were compelled to sell him their produce at shamefully low prices because their trucks would probably break down on the way to a more profitable market in Reggio. He stood up slowly as Falcone came toward him. "What do you want?"

Falcone was a lean man, bent as a windbreak tree, with thinning hair and watery grayish eyes. He began with an equally watery smile, saying, "*Amico* Claudio—"

"*Signor* Bianchi to you, thief." The last several weeks had done nothing for Bianchi's civility.

"*Bene*, *Signor* Bianchi, then." Falcone appeared to have a brief coughing fit before he could get the next words out. "I understand that you have recently had a . . ." More coughing. "Ah—a *visitor* . . ."

Does everybody in the whole world know everything about me? "So?"

Falcone's long, pocked face seemed to change in an odd way, becoming somehow more defined, as his eyes focused on Bianchi's eyes. He said, "I know those people. I have . . . had dealings with them."

"I am sure you have. Get to the point and go, Falcone."

Falcone's face broke open, revealing a face that Bianchi had never seen before: truly broken, frightened beyond coherence, yet actually—incredibly—concerned for the safety of another person, one who was not even family. "Bianchi, you do not say *no* to those people. It is very brave of you—I admire it—I wish I could be as brave as you—"

"I am not brave," Bianchi said. "I am stubborn and stupid, or I would not have kept on selling my vegetables to you all these years. But the day I get that Studebaker transmission fixed—"

"Bianchi, they will kill you! They will hurt you first, in all the ways they know, and then they will kill you, like swatting a fly. Like swatting a fly! You call me a thief, but I am trying to help you—"

Bianchi raised a hand, both to silence him, and in something approaching a peaceful gesture. "I know you are, Falcone, and I appreciate it." It took a serious struggle to get the words out, but he went on. "It was . . . good of you. But they do not really want this *porca miseria* farm of mine. They want the unicorns they think are living on my land. When they finally realize that there are no unicorns—" he looked levelly into the gray eyes—"that there never were unicorns, that same moment they will lose all interest—"

"But they will *not* believe, and they will not wait! They are the *'Ndrangheta*, Bianchi—they like to make examples of people who cross them! They may decide to kill you anyway, just because you will not sell them your farm. They may!" Falcone was very nearly in tears.

Bianchi put a hand on his bony shoulder. "Go home, my criminal friend. We all do what we must do—even unicorns, I suppose. I will be all right, one way or another. Go back to robbing poor farmers . . . and thank you. I thank you, Falcone."

Watching the gaunt, stooped figure trudging back to his funereal Fiat—*and we know who paid for that car, don't we, old friend?*—Bianchi felt loneliness descend upon him like an old coat he had owned in his youth: a blue woolen coat so often soaked by mountain rains that it never truly dried, even in the sun, and had no warmth in it to provide him. *I am afraid. I am more frightened than Falcone, and what sort of thing is that for a grown man to admit? I wish Giovanna were here. No, I am glad she is not here—there is too much danger now, what am I thinking? I must order her not ever to come. I wish I did not wish she were here.*

Whether due to the rumors of threats from the 'Ndrangheta, or simply to the boredom that Bianchi had so long predicted, the flood both of hunters and media commentators definitely dwindled in the ensuing days and weeks. The weather warmed; the big tourist hotels and resorts down at sea level were hiring, as were other people's farms— Bianchi was known for almost never employing other hands than his own. There were far fewer television features and interviews, and almost no overflights by news helicopters or surveillance drones. Even the animal-rights people appeared less often on his doorstep with their loudspeakers and their lawyers. Bianchi was glad of this, and hoped that the monster and his fellows had taken notice.

But he knew better, and could not help but be glad of that as well. For *La Signora* and her son, strangely obdurate as himself, remained as clearly present as ever, if only during the twilight hours at dusk and dawn, and not always visibly, even to Bianchi. But at this point, he could feel their nearness, whether waking or dreaming, and sometimes thought that he could walk straight out of his house in the night, with his eyes closed, and find his way to them. *Actually, I would probably fall into a hole and break my leg—but maybe not . . .*

Giorgio Malatesta, the garage owner, also came to visit, on the same errand as Falcone, and so did Domenico Amendola, the butcher, who was called *Pazzo* by everyone, although he was not crazy at all. Bianchi berated the one for his shameless substitution of Albanian parts for good Italian ones, the other for the prices he charged for dubious rabbits and hens who could have remembered more prime ministers than he. He also thanked them, as graciously as he knew how, for risking the wrath of the 'Ndrangheta on his behalf, which sent them both scuttling home without even stopping for coffee. Bianchi was sourly amused by this; but he was touched, as well, as he had been with Matteo Falcone. *They are old men, and they are who they are—it is wrong of me to expect them to be different, this late in their lives. I am old, too, and I don't change either.*

Yet that was wrong too: he had changed, and knew it, though more clearly than he could isolate the cause. Obstinate as he had been all his life, he would ordinarily never have dared, no more than Malatesta or Falcone, to defy the gangs who ran Calabria with more brutal thoroughness than today's Mafia ran Sicily. *What on earth got into me, in the name of God? Why did "Fuck you, with your fucking cowboy-movie cigars" come into my mind so naturally? Because of the unicorns? Because I helped a unicorn into this world, and that makes me responsible to them? To myself? Responsible to be a hero? God's burning asshole, if I had known that!*

Was it her?

Did I sign my own death warrant because of a woman far too young for me—practically a girl— who has funny golden specks down in her green eyes, and thinks she can drive a motorcycle, which will kill her as surely as the 'Ndrangheta? And who arches, all unknowing, like a cat if you touch the back of her neck? If that is so, I would surely be better off dead.

But I do wish she were here.

On those moments—always at night now—when *La Signora* chose to show herself to him, glowing on a hilltop like the rising moon, he sensed a restiveness in her, a disquiet that made him wonder if, as birds do in autumn or the earliest spring, she were not readying herself to fly. The black colt was not always with her; indeed, Bianchi had once or twice glimpsed him alone, casting about in different directions in short bursts of speed, then shaking his head and racing off on another path: a single slash of pure blackness against a blue-black night sky. The horn had not grown as much as he had; *perhaps he will shed it every year, like antlers, and every spring it will be bigger, longer, sharper. Something else I will never know.*

He wrote a poem about that, about not knowing so many things in a life. The poem was a failure, as far as he was ever concerned; he felt so about most of the poems he wrote during that time. Which was odd, when he thought much about it, because it was really a good time, taken all in all. Everything he had planted during the strange, rainy winter was coming up strong and healthy, despite the trampling invasions of the unicorn hunters. Giovanna had absolutely refused his warnings, and kept bringing him her warm, laughing presence—though hardly ever any mail—every Friday in the blue van.

And the monster, the Toscano-smoking ambassador of the *'Ndrangheta*, had at least kept his word: there were no threatening telephone calls—no calls of any kind—and no further visits. He never allowed himself to grow less vigilant; but happiness is the old enemy of watchfulness, and Bianchi was practically happy. Growling contentment is not the same thing, but he hadn't known.

The dinner that he cooked for Giovanna was the first meal he had ever cooked for anyone; working up to the invitation took him a good deal longer than the execution. He made *ciambatta,* which involves stewed eggplant, potatoes, tomatoes, peppers, and the matchless red onions of Calabria, and which was the only dish he trusted himself to make for company. There was *ricci di donna* pasta in tomato sauce, and a bottle of the red Cirò that he had taken in trade for helping Vittorio Bava to repair his son-in-law's chimney. He put flowers in whatever vases and empty jars he had, and set them wherever they seemed to brighten the little farmhouse, and he swept the floor and put last night's dishes away, and he forbade Garibaldi and all three cats entry for the night, telling them firmly, "The nights are warmer now, you can sleep perfectly well in the barn. You have become so spoiled!" But he petted them all, by way of apology, before he turned them outside.

Giovanna arrived riding pillion on her friend

Silvana's Vespa. She hopped off, kissed Silvana on both cheeks, and walked straight into Bianchi's arms where he stood waiting at his door. Silvana, watching, waved with knowing cheerfulness as she drove away, but Giovanna did not turn her head.

Embracing her was somewhat awkward, due to the backpack slung from her shoulders. Bianchi asked, "How will you get home?"

"Silvana will come and get me in the morning. This is all very exciting for her."

"Oh," Bianchi said. "Well. I made dinner."

"And I am sure it will be wonderful." She took his hand and led him to his own bedroom, which, from that moment, seemed forever like someone else's.

Staring at her as she tugged her woolen shirt off over her head, he said, "Child, I remember you when you were learning to walk—"

"Yes, I know, you keep telling me." The sweet, shifting dance of her shoulders and collarbones made the skin of his face tingle. "And it is plain that if we delay any longer, you will simply crumble away, so we had better get to business, don't you think?" Naked, she rose on her toes when she kissed him, which was flattering, but hardly necessary.

Later, her voice muffled against his chest, she murmured, "You must never call me *child* again. I will slap you if you do. Besides, you are only twenty-three-and-a-half years older than I am. Romano told me."

"Romano. What will you tell *him* tomorrow?"

"Oh, he thinks that I am staying with Silvana. She will come and get me early, before he comes with your mail. We know his schedule to the second." She tangled her legs with his. "Sleep a little. We will have your lovely dinner at midnight."

And so they did, with Bianchi in his father's old bathrobe, and Giovanna in the flowered nightgown she had brought in her backpack. Sitting across from him, with her legs curled under her, the gold-flecked green eyes happily heavy and her hair like a bird's nest, she pronounced the meal exquisite, the flowers perfect, the Ciro the best wine she had ever tasted, and his ancient robe adorable. When he asked hesitantly, "Have you been . . . thinking about this for a long time?" she giggled like a schoolgirl at first; but then she looked down at the table and nodded. He said, "About *me*?"

"And what is so astonishing about that, Signor Claudio Bianchi? Unicorns come to you all the

117

time—why shouldn't a woman?" Her eyes were not at all heavy then, but wickedly tender. Bianchi looked away from them.

He said, "I was married once."

"Yes. Romano has told me. And she left you. So?"

"She was right to leave me. I was not good at being married."

"Bianchi," she said. "Claudio. Marriage isn't like football, like *bocce*. One isn't *good* at it, nobody has a special gift. You stumble along, and if there is enough love—" she smiled at him—"you learn."

Bianchi got up from the table abruptly enough that Giovanna's eyes widened. He turned in a circle, like a captive animal—a bear or an elephant—and then he stood leaning with his hands on the back of his chair. "There is no love in me. There is nothing to be learned. She would have stayed if there were, but she knew. I am just telling you now."

"A unicorn has stayed."

Bianchi was silent for a moment. "*La Signora* chose my farm because she felt it would be a safe place to have her baby. Not because of me."

"You think not?" Giovanna's expression was a curious mixture of exasperation and affectionate amusement. "You think a unicorn would not know—would not *know*—who would come out of his house in a storm to help her in her trouble? To perhaps save her child's life? You think unicorns don't know such things, Bianchi?"

Bianchi turned his back to her, his shaggy head lowering. "Unicorns know nothing. Otherwise she would never have let me near her."

Giovanna waited, unspeaking. Bianchi was doing something with his hands that she had seen him do before, the fingers of the left hand hooking over the right knuckles, squeezing rhythmically, so hard that she winced to see it. Bianchi said, "You don't know anything, either."

"Well, I know exactly where you are ticklish," she said. "How many people have ever known that?"

When he finally sat down at the table again, she reached for his hand, but he pulled it away, folding his arms in front of him. He said, "I pulled another child from its mother's belly once. Long ago. So long ago that it feels as though it happened to someone else. But it happened to me—and to her."

Giovanna placed her own hands flat on the table, close to his, but not touching. "Your child died?"

Bianchi nodded. "If there had been a doctor . . . But it was night, and we had no money, and after all, I knew how to deliver a calf, a puppy—a goat, even. She was safe with me."

"And she never forgave—" Giovanna stopped herself, the green eyes widening. Slowly she said, "No . . . no, *she* forgave you—but you . . . *ay*, Bianchi. Bianchi."

"It was long ago, I told you," he answered indifferently. "One goes on. One gets . . . used to things."

As if I could ever get used to your touch, ever get used to your lovely cold feet in my bed—get used to another person, ever again, at this table where I eat my meals and write my poems. Get used to the way I will feel when you leave in the morning.

"But you do not go on," she said. "You stay exactly where you were, that night when your child died." Bianchi sat motionless, but he clenched his hands on his wrists, and she could see that he was shivering. After a silence filled with each other's eyes, she said in a surprisingly small voice, "My friends call me *Gio*. You could call me that, if you like."

"Gio," Bianchi said. "Gio. All right."

She fell asleep as soon as they went back to bed, snoring daintily on his shoulder and holding him so tightly that it was almost painful. But when he said, "She did not leave me because of the baby, but because of what you said—because I could not, could not . . ." she woke up immediately and answered, "*E allora?* More fool she."

"No," he said. "No, she was not a fool, she was wise to leave," but Giovanna was asleep again.

Bianchi stayed awake all night, inhaling her closeness, listening to the soft sounds her body made, thinking, *can you write a poem about someone's snores? About trying not to sneeze when her hair tickles my nose? About that one tiny, barely audible fart against my leg? What will I write at my kitchen table, now that she has been there, drinking my wine and eating the dinner I made for her? Late to be discovering all this, Bianchi—all this that children know about these days. Very, very late . . .*

There would have been time for breakfast, as he had envisioned, but for the spirit in which she awoke. They were barely dressed before they heard the sputter of the motorscooter. Giovanna peeped through the door, waved to Silvana while stuffing her nightgown into her backpack, and kissed Bianchi hard enough that their teeth clattered together and brought blood from her lower lip. She touched her finger to the blood, and then to the tip of his nose. "*There*, so you'll know I will come back," and she was out and gone, smiling at him from the back of the Vespa. Silvana waved too.

Bianchi moved slowly for the rest of the day. He let the three cows out to graze, fed the pigs and checked the security of their pen, as he did every day, and irrigated his fields and trees for the first time since the rains ended, reminding himself to replace two of the water hoses. But for all that, he was still absent from his activity, not thinking even about Giovanna . . . *Gio* . . . but rather savoring the calmness in his skin that had nothing to do with work, or spring, or poetry. "*So you'll know I will come back* . . ." Sometimes he smiled vaguely, just for the sensation of the bruise on his own mouth.

Romano, who arrived with an electricity bill and a new Dell'Acqua fashion catalogue, said after one glance, "It is obviously an epic that has carried you off. Something about the days of the Carbonari? About football? Unicorns?" He turned in all directions as he spoke, gazing hopefully everywhere but at Bianchi.

"No poem." Bianchi replied. "No unicorns."

"Perhaps that would be a good thing," Romano said. "I have been hearing . . ." He did not finish, but began rooting earnestly in his mail pouch, as though in futile search of an actual letter. The back of his neck looked to Bianchi as young and vulnerable as his sister's neck.

"You have heard what? Tell me." Bianchi's stomach knew what was coming, but he himself needed the words.

"Those people . . ." Romano still did not turn.

"What people? The 'Ndrangheta? Say it, Romano."

"Barbato," Romano mumbled. "The one who sells flowers on the Via Cavour? Marco, his son, he's not *in* the 'Ndrangheta, you understand, but he does favors for them sometimes—just a few favors." He did turn to Bianchi then, and his face was more taut and strained than the older man had ever seen it. "But it will be all right, if the unicorns are really gone. I can spread the word—I go everywhere, you know that—and they won't want your land then. I can do that."

Bianchi put his hands on the postman's shoulders. "*Pace, fratello mio.* The *'Ndrangheta* have had plenty of time to come after me, and they have not done so. They are drug traffickers, arms dealers, extortionists—why would they waste time on rumors of a couple of mythical beasts perhaps seen on one ignorant farmer's wretched few hectares? Whatever else they are, they are not stupid."

But the words sounded bodiless even to him, and he could have spoken Romano's response along with him. "No—but you are, if you think they have finished with you. They have only begun, Bianchi."

Cherubino, who was afraid of the mail van, came up as it rumbled away and nudged familiarly against Bianchi, on the chance of there being something for him in the faded work shirt. Bianchi scratched him absently behind the horns, thinking, *would they hurt the animals? Even the 'Ndrangheta surely wouldn't hurt a three-legged cat.* He realized that his hands were cold and trembling, and he shoved them into his pocket. *Yes, they would. Yes, they would. And they would hurt her, if she were here . . .*

This time, when they spoke that night, he made it an order, not a warning. "You are not to come here again—not ever, not for any reason. If I see you here, I will send you right away, even if there is no trouble. Do you understand me?" When she did not answer, he repeated, "Do you understand me? Gio?" He was still oddly shy about using the intimate nickname.

"I am nodding," she said flatly. "I am not saying *yes*. Do you understand the difference?"

"Oh, yes. Once I would not have, but since I have known you . . ." And then the name, and the words, did come, like a prison break from his caged heart. "Gio . . . Gio . . . I have lived all my life in this country. I know what I have, and what I can do without. I know what I will never have, and I know how to tell myself that I never wanted it anyway. But if something were to happen to you . . ." He stopped, because his mouth was very dry, and when he tried to breathe, nothing happened. "That I could not endure, if something bad happened to you. So you stay away, that's all, *è tutto*. Gio—*bella*—stay away."

He was about to hang up the phone before it dropped from his shaking hand, when he heard her say quietly, "Yes. I love you too, Claudio."

"*Giobella*," he said, when he could speak, "I think I will always call you that. No one else calls you Giobella, do they?"

"No—no one." She said it laughingly, but there were tears in her voice. "No one but Claudio Bianchi."

That afternoon, suddenly angry to find himself looking constantly around him with the quick, anxious twitches of a deer in his garden, he went searching for his father's old shotgun in the attic. It took him some while: the Bianchis had never been much concerned with hunting, and their family feuds tended to be carried on verbally over decades. As his Uncle Vincenzo had often said, before he lost all interest in any conversation but with his chickens, "Dead people can't hear what you're yelling at them."

He finally discovered the shotgun—double-barreled, rusty around the breech, but apparently functional—half-hidden behind an old-fashioned clothespress, with a small bag of cartridges hanging from the trigger guard. *Buckshot? Birdshot? What is a man who can't tell the difference on sight doing with such a thing? Besides, it would most likely blow my head off before they do.* His solitary laughter was kept from self-mocking melodrama only by a fit of sneezing. *Beat the 'Ndrangheta off with your manure shovel, Bianchi. Better yet, an insulting poem—that should put them to flight. Giobella, your man—if that can really be what I am—is no better a guardian than my poor old toothless Garibaldi. Yet he has been brave as a bear in his time, defending his home, and so must I be now.*

He set the shotgun back where he had found it, and went downstairs, where he discovered on his doorstep the body of Third Cat, the nameless feral one who had appeared, years ago, as strangely and suddenly as the unicorn, and stayed on to eat his food and avoid his touch. The blunt brindle head had been nearly cut off and the belly split open; the intestines were still steaming in the cooling air. In death the old cat had voided its bowels, and that also was so fresh that the murder must have occurred only moments before, while he had been up in the attic, playing with guns.

"*Ay*, cat," he said softly, kneeling over the ruined body. "And you never told me your name." He picked the dead animal up, regardless of blood and shit, and stood staring at the imprint of heavy shoes in the churned earth. "You fought them, didn't you?" he asked the cat. "You left your mark on them." A rage he had rarely known took hold of him then, and for longer than he ever remembered he cursed the footprints and the horizon they led back to, until his vision blurred and his voice gave out.

Then he found a spade and walked slowly—a one-man funeral cortege—to the nearby hollow where *La Signora* had chosen to give birth to her black colt. He buried Third Cat there, marking the grave with a small white stone.

None of the other animals had been harmed, though the cow Gianetta had developed a runny eye that warranted attention. Bianchi determinedly put in his usual afternoon of spading, wheeling, spreading, weeding, and loaming, despite a sudden new flurry of scholars, romantics, and venture capitalists—*what else are the 'Ndrangheta, really?*—as well as a return visit from a pair of television personalities who had plagued him for weeks since *La Signora's* existence had first become rumored. Bianchi was more polite to them than he had been, having had more practice; but all the same, he was wearier when they left than a full day's work should have made him.

With them gone, he called the cows in to be milked, put away his tools and put food out for the cats and Garibaldi, and sat down on the old wicker chair that Giovanna had urged him to bring up from the barn, "just in case a friend might actually wish to stay and talk with you. You never know, Bianchi." Personally, he felt that the chair offered much too open an invitation to interviewers; but he found himself doing it nevertheless, because she had asked.

The unicorns came to him in the slow, slanting light of late afternoon. He was too tired and downhearted to rise, even for unicorns, but sat motionless, watching them walk toward him, the white-golden and the black, shining with their own moonlight, even in the sun of the *mezzogiorno*, their cloven hooves making no sound. They came all the way to where he was and stood as still as he, and he put his hand on both their heads without fearing to alarm them. He said, "Third Cat is dead."

La Signora looked into his eyes, as she had done before, but this time Bianchi looked back and lost himself in a bright wilderness: a forest filled with glowing, shifting shadows, where nothing threatened, but nothing he knew applied, nothing he recognized held its shape for long. He felt himself altering, amending, as he wandered there—for how long?—until he had to make himself return while there was still a *himself* to command. *And that is why men hunt unicorns, and why they will always kill them when they capture them. Not the beauty, not the magic of the horn . . . because of what lives and waits in the eyes. Finally I understand.*

"I have asked before why you stay on, for all the trouble, and the danger. Whatever you are waiting for, it must be very important to you. All I know to say to you now is that bad people will be coming here soon, looking for you. You do not know them.

These people are different from the fools and clowns and silly children who have been hunting you over my land all this time. They are clever, they are organized, and once they have their hands on you, they will use you, use your existence, in every way they can. I cannot protect you, and I do not know how to advise you, so I can only beg you to go away now. As I have begged my ... someone as important to me as any unicorn to stay away from me."

La Signora did not move, nor did the black colt. A sudden wave of cold bitterness overtook Bianchi, and he stood up from the wicker chair and shouted, "Everyone I care about should just stay away from me! People—animals—everyone, all of you! Do what you want, but stay away!"

The unicorn did a strange thing then: she lowered her head and touched him with her horn, lightly, glancingly, on his left shoulder, almost as though she were making him a knight of some order whose sense and purpose he would never know. It hurt him, though the point of the horn never broke the skin, or even penetrated his frayed old workshirt; it hurt so that he cried aloud and thought that he must surely vomit from the pain. Then it stopped hurting.

Bianchi said, "Oh." After that he said, "But I can't." He touched his shoulder. He said, "I have to." He turned without saying anything more, walked into his house, sat down at the kitchen table, *where we had our dinner at midnight, a life ago,* and began to write a poem.

It was not about the unicorns; or if it was, he never knew it. Nor was it about Giovanna Muscari, though he meant it to be. Poems come as they will, and when; and this one insisted on being a calm farewell to Cherubino, and to Garibaldi, Sophia and Mezzanotte, and to Gianetta, Martina, and Lucia as well, and to the pigs. The poem asked them all to take care of one another as best they might be able—he worried especially about the cows not being milked, *but Romano will know, Romano will surely hear them calling when he comes*—and if they kept some memory of him at all, to remember that he had loved them.

He was very precise about it all, addressing everything that had shared his life, even in small ways. He urged his grapevines to guard themselves against crown gall, shoot necrosis, and spiral nematodes; reminded his apple orchard to keep cold, and the deer to keep their word and continue leaving his tomatoes and his vegetable beds alone. At the end, he wrote only two lines to Giovanna.

When he finished, he was sharply disappointed, seeing it as far more of a last will than a real poem. He considered destroying it, but then decided that since he did not have a will of any sort—nor any heir, no better than crazy Uncle Vincenzo—it should be left where it could be discovered after his death, for whatever use it might be to anyone. So he put it away in the desk with the poems, because Giovanna knew where he kept those.

He had become strangely calm, and wondered at it in a distant way. *If this is happening because she touched me with her horn, that is a splendid and remarkable thing, of course, but I wish that she had made me bulletproof instead. That would be practical, at least.* He completed his evening tasks later than usual, sat in the kitchen for a while with his pipe and the last of the red Ciro, and at last went to bed. Remembering when he was too sleepy to get up again that he had forgotten to call Giovanna. He smiled drowsily, thinking about her . . .

. . . and woke up just as the door crashed in with a splintering squeal of hinges, and he was on the floor, being kicked scientifically and enthusiastically by all the feet in the world. The work was actually being done by only three pairs, but he did not realize this until he had been hauled upright a couple of times, slammed against his bed, and knocked down again, so that the kicking could continue. Somewhere in the process, he struck out in the darkness, felt a nose give, heard a gasping obscenity, and doubled over from a hammer-blow to his stomach. He clung to his assailant with all his strength, clawing for a grip on arms and shoulders he could not see, fearing to go down again. None of them said a word—a message was simply being delivered—and all he could think, as much as he could think, was *thank God she isn't here . . . oh, thank God . . . thank God . . .*

*. . . and then the motorcycle—Romano, he bought that used muffler from Malatesta—*and the beating stopped at the sound . . . and she *was* there, raging among them through the broken door, swinging a tire iron like a flaming sword and screaming like a maniac. The 'Ndrangheta had no time to prepare for such an attack; in the close quarters the iron got home with every swing, and Giovanna drove them from one wall to the other, round and round,

until they blundered outside and fled, lurching and limping, to the car that Bianchi had never heard arrive. She did not pursue, but dropped the tire iron and ran to him, dropping to her knees to catch him as he sagged, cursing steadily and fluently, and crying through it all. In the end, it was Bianchi who had to hold her.

"I am all right," he kept telling her. "Giobella, I am really all right, they did not injure me much." But even as he said it, he retched thinly in her lap, and she had the light on and the nightshirt off, and was prowling around him, assessing his bruises. There was almost no blood, except from his mouth—the 'Ndrangheta know their business— but everything hurt, and would hurt worse the next day, and for many days after that. Giovanna went back to cursing as she heated water and found clean cloths to wash him thoroughly. She only started crying again after she got him into bed and climbed in beside him.

"How did you know?" he managed to ask her. "It isn't Friday."

"It is Wednesday night, or Thursday morning by now. And you did not call, and . . . *non sono sicuro*—something felt wrong . . ."

As I would feel it . . . "So you stole your brother's motorcycle, which you do not know how to drive—"

"I did *not* steal it. Stealing is when you don't bring it back. And I only fell once. Well, twice, but that one was the truck's fault. No, that is just a small scrape, leave it alone. What matters is that I got here."

"Yes," he said. "Thank you, Giobella." After a moment he added, still somewhat shy about it, "Giobella *mia.*"

She was silent for such a while that he thought she must have fallen asleep. But presently she said, "They will come back. You cannot be alone when they do."

"It will be different this time. Perhaps they will send that man I first met, the one I told you about—"

"No, it will be worse! *Ascoltame*, Bianchi, listen! They have lost face tonight, they have been shamed—"

"That was your doing alone, not mine. God knows, it was not mine."

"Which makes it worse, because now it is not simply a matter of business, not just about unicorns, land, papers they want you to sign. Now it is *la vendetta!*" The word hissed in the night, in the bed, like an angry snake. "I will not let you be alone up here."

"And I will not let you . . ." It was quickly becoming painful to get words out through split, blood-encrusted lips "You have risked enough, woman, *enough*! They may already have been asking questions about you, about us—if they do not know tonight who it was on the motorcycle, they will tomorrow. No more. Not even on Fridays."

In the end—and it took all the rest of the night—they came to an agreement which satisfied neither of them. For the sake of propriety, Giovanna would arrive with her friend Silvana on every Tuesday evening, and go home the same way in the morning, as she had done before, returning on Friday for her regular mail delivery. "It is not that Romano doesn't know. He knew what was happening before I did—as I told you, sometimes he understands more than you would expect from a brother. But if he does not ever admit to me, or to you, that he knows, then he is not lying when he tells other people that he does not know. Men amaze me."

But she agreed, or seemed to agree, that she

would not come to his house on any whim or impulse, even if by some chance he did not phone her; nor would she stay any night but Tuesday. He, in his turn, promised faithfully to report the attack to the police—even though neither one expected any result but paperwork—but refused firmly to visit a doctor. "I have been hurt worse by donkeys, cows, my own tools. Nothing is broken, nothing is damaged inside. If something else starts hurting . . . *bene*, yes, then I will go. Will that content you?"

"No, that is just stupid. But we will let it alone—for now—on one condition. One condition only." She paused, waiting for a response. "Do you not want to know what that condition is?"

"The poems I have been writing lately are not very good. I should tell you that."

Giovanna was lying on her side, her chin resting on one closed fist. "No, this has nothing to do with poetry." She smiled at him: the particular burst of challenging mischief that he had seen, once in a while, on the reserved, serious face of the child he remembered. She said, "You must allow me to buy you a pair of pajamas." Bianchi stared at her. "If you are going to continue offending people who will continue to drag you from your bed at all hours and . . . and attack you, then at least you must greet them wearing something more suitable than that horrible nightshirt. For the sake of your dignity."

Bianchi gaped for a moment more, then began to laugh for what felt to him like the first time in a great many years. "So now I am not dressing for myself, not even for you. Now I am dressing for the 'Ndranghetu. Perhaps I should ask the cows for their opinion of my underwear. Or Cherubino, better; he ate some of it once, off the drying line. And Mezzanotte—he slept wrapped in that nightshirt when he was a kitten. Does he not deserve a vote, too?"

He saw the green eyes grow large, and quickly put his arms around her. "Giobella, I am sorry for making fun of you, please forgive me. But they are not going to attack me like that again. That was the first message—" he did not mention Third Cat— "the second one will be different. I do not really think I will need to dress for it."

"The second could be a fire!" she cried out. "The second could be a bomb, dynamite, a single shot while you are milking your cows. What will you do then, Bianchi? What will *I* do?"

She was actually shaking him, with her hands painfully tight on his shoulders. He caught them, kissed them both, held them in one of his own large hands that had never been made for writing poetry. He said quietly, "You will have to finish milking the cows."

They repaired the door together, picked up whatever had not been broken, and threw away the rest of the wreckage. Breakfast was *caffe latte* and toast, spread with the last of the preserves that had been a recent gift from Matteo Falcone, for the lean merchant's own strange reasons. They ate in near-complete silence, and then Bianchi walked out with her to her brother's motorcycle. It was parked precariously on damp, yielding earth, and he could see deep boot-heel marks where she had leaped to the ground and come charging to his aid like an avenging angel. He said in a mix of wonder and mild reproof, "You must have been carrying that tire iron in your hand all the way—there is no saddlebag big enough to hold it. That was very dangerous."

"I left it on the bed for you." She held him very tightly, and though her breathing was harsh and irregular, she was not crying. "Please do not get killed, you stubborn, foolish man. I am too young to be hurting for the rest of my life."

"And I am too young and silly for you. But you will be my Giobella for the rest of *my* life. So be very, very careful going home, because you don't know how to drive. And call me when you get there, *capisci?*" She promised.

Watching the motorcycle wobble out of sight down the dirt road—her friend Silvana took the curve much faster on her Vespa—he felt an absurdly wrenching urge to go after her in the old Studebaker, to make certain that she reached home safely. *You cannot protect her from anything, Bianchi. Not from herself, not from the 'Ndrangheta—not from her stupid, idiotic, miraculous love for you. The best you can do for her is to try not to get killed. And hope she forgets about the pajamas.*

He did call the police, keeping his own word, and weary *Tenente* Esposito came out to take a full report, drink two cups of coffee, and tell him, as they both knew he would, "Bianchi, what do you imagine we can do about the *'Ndrangheta* that the police of five, six countries have not been able to do? I can send someone out a couple of times a week to sit and drink coffee with you, as I do, but beyond that . . ." He shrugged as expressively as only someone who has spent an entire life in southernmost Italy can do. "Of course, if you were to sell your farm, now, and move down into town . . ." Bianchi raised his eyebrows without replying, and *Tenente* Esposito did not bother to finish the sentence. "Well, you have friends in town—even you—and you have neighbors, everyone has neighbors. You could alert them, they could organize a patrol . . ."

"Aldo Frascati," Bianchi said. "Yes, he would be thrilled to defend me from the *'Ndrangheta*. I will start with him, and then I will enlist Madame Leonora. More coffee?" *Tenente* Esposito indicated that that would be very nice.

As a gesture, or as a sort of charm—both are taken quite seriously in Calabria—Bianchi began keeping Giovanna's tire iron close to him at all times, even carrying it with him when he went out to work the farm. The shotgun meant nothing to him, nor he to it, but the tire iron had been brought for his protection by someone who loved him. He told Giovanna that he did this, because she believed devoutly in such things; but not that he slept with it cold by his side on nights when he was most lonely for his green-eyed girl. On some mornings he woke up gripping it tightly, as though preparing to face further attackers; but if he had been dreaming of the 'Ndrangheta, he never recalled the dreams. And the 'Ndrangheta did not come.

Neither did the unicorns, singly or together. Bianchi continued to believe strongly that he would have known if they were no longer present on his land: as he tried to explain to Giovanna, "The air would be different. When I think about them, I can feel the air ripple and shiver around me, and I understand that they are somewhere near. Does that sound foolish to you?"

Instead of answering the question directly, she asked him, "And when you think of me? What happens then?"

Very gravely, Bianchi responded, "When I think about you, sometimes I cannot breathe." She looked up at him and hugged his arm, saying nothing at all.

On all evenings except Tuesdays, when she came on her friend's motorscooter, he would sit still in the wicker chair, neither reading nor writing, but waiting to feel the unicorns, without expecting to see them. He would close his eyes, whisper *"Vieni, vieni"* into the warm appleblossom breezes, without caring whether or not they carried his plea to two pairs, white and black, of silken pointed ears, and listen for them with the skin of his face, which was where he most often felt their reality. Sometimes he fell asleep like that, and always woke up smiling.

During that time, he was regularly surprised by more visitors from town than he had ever been accustomed to receive. Rossi, Dallessandro, Falcone again, wheezy-voiced Frascati—even Madame Leonora, stately in the sidecar of young De Santis, her police-officer great-nephew. All brought gifts of one sort or another, according to their professions, and all came bearing equally varied warnings and advice. Bianchi should sell the farm to the 'Ndrangheta and move down into town . . . no, he should simply leave town altogether and emigrate to Canada or New Zealand . . . no, he should electrify his fences and mine his property so completely with grenades and dynamite that the first step any gangster took on it would be his last in this world . . . no, he should hire bodyguards, gangsters of his own, to patrol his farm night and day . . . Killer dogs were also mentioned.

To the cats he marveled, "I have never been so popular as now, in the hour of my doom. I must remember this. What a rare thing."

On days when Romano delivered the mail, he spoke far less than usual, and seemed to regard Bianchi with a curious new mixture of admiration, puzzlement, and deep misgiving, the latter most often expressed in the corner of his eye. When Bianchi challenged him directly to say what was on his mind, Romano would only shrug, flap his arms vaguely, and go off shaking his head. Bianchi would stare after him, half-amused, half as bewildered as he.

Finally, one afternoon when an exasperated Bianchi had followed him to the mail van, pressing him sharply for an answer, Romano turned on him, red and white with anger by turns. "You are going to make my sister a widow before she is ever married. If you want to stretch your neck out on the block and wait for the *'Ndrangheta* to chop your head off . . . well, that is your own stupid business—but at least have the decency to tell her not to love you so much. *Order* her not to love you, Bianchi—do that much, if you do nothing more." There were no tears in his eyes, but he was trembling, and his nose was running. "No, don't do that, of course not, she would never take orders from God and Santo Michele together. But if you love *her*, then stop sitting here with no gun, no friends, no police, writing your poems and feeding your pigs. Protect your woman, Bianchi, if you won't protect yourself."

He scrambled clumsily and angrily into the van, and was away without a wave or a backward glance.

"I think he wishes that he had never taught you to drive," he said to Giovanna when the Vespa dropped her off that evening. "So much might have been avoided."

"Oh, I would have learned," she replied lightly. "And I already knew where you lived." She chuckled against him, rubbing her head against his arm like a cat. "Silvana was going to teach me, and I was always watching my brothers." She frowned then, thoughtfully enough that the dark brows became a straight bar. "Something is wrong with Silvana, I think. Perhaps a man, perhaps family—they are a little strange, her people. Silvana is the only one of them I could ever . . ." She shrugged abruptly and dropped the subject. "She doesn't talk to me as much, and today she kept looking at me . . . oddly. I am probably imagining it."

"She may be frightened for you," Bianchi said quietly. "As your brother is—as I am. She may know something, and be afraid to speak. This is Calabria, after all."

"She would not dare!" The eyebrows now seemed to melt into each other. "If she heard or saw something that might be dangerous to you, or even picked up the rumor of a rumor that someone had said something to someone else, and she did not tell me, she would be better off in the hands of the 'Ndrangheta." She glared at him with comical ferocity. "So would you be, if you knew something and tried to spare me or shield me. I have a right to say that, Bianchi."

"I will shield you from nothing," he promised her. "Rather, I will hide behind you." She continued to glare, suspecting that he was mocking her; then saw that he was not, and let her small face ease into soft laughter. Her laugh always sounded to Bianchi like green leaves rustling against each other.

On a Tuesday evening, while she was putting away the dinner dishes—never having cooked for anyone in his life, it was more exciting than he could ever explain to be preparing as simple a dish as *baccalà al pomodoro* for them to eat together— she said over her shoulder, "But they could have gone away, you know. How long has it been since you have seen them? Can you really be so certain?"

"It is not important what I believe," Bianchi replied. "What the 'Ndrangheta believe—that is what matters."

Giovanna turned from the dishes, and he shrugged. "I think perhaps whether the unicorns are still here or not does not matter so much to them anymore. *La vendetta,* now . . ."

Giovanna set down the dish towel, so gently and deliberately that the effect was more fierce than if she had hurled it across the kitchen. In a similarly quiet voice, she remarked, "I think you should know that when they shoot you down on your own doorstep, I will not wear mourning. I may not even go to your funeral."

"*Va bene,*" Bianchi agreed amiably. "The *Tenente* has already assured me that he would come, and I am sure Malatesta would not miss it for a fortune. I may even get that thief Falcone, and if old Frascati's arthritis is not bothering him too greatly—"

She was across the kitchen and at him before he could put up his hands to defend himself, beating at him with the same fury with which she had routed the 'Ndrangheta thugs. "You joke!" she gasped. "I can stand anything but this stupid, stupid joking!" A sudden explosion of helpless, furious tears rendered her almost speechless. "Bianchi, they really will kill you, they will burn this house over your head—"

Bianchi caught her flailing hands and held them to his cheek. "But not tonight," he said. He put his arms around her. "Not tonight. Come."

He led her outside, and they sat in the twilight, snuggled into the old wicker chair, each with a glass of white Ciro, and Bianchi's worn brown jacket around Giovanna's shoulders. After a time, she said softly, "See, now, this moment, we are just like ordinary people, people who are not afraid, not looking for unicorns, but only keeping each other warm on a spring evening. Nothing more, nothing less."

Bianchi was silent for a little while before he answered her. "Do not make any mistake about me. This is very important—I do not ever want you to imagine that I am a fearless warrior, indifferent to death, because I am nothing of the kind. And yet—" he hesitated, plainly reaching for words that he had never spoken to her before. "She touched me, you know, Giobella—*La Signora*. With her horn . . . *here*. I told you that?" Giovanna nodded, her mouth set for whatever she might hear, but her green eyes wide and waiting. "I did. Yes. Well, it hurt me at the time—it hurt terribly, like a brand, the way we do with cattle, horses, so that everyone will know they are ours."

He brought her hand to his left shoulder, and she pulled back, feeling the heat through the worn fabric. "Yes, just so," he said again. "Ever since then . . . ever since then, I do not seem to care about being afraid. Somewhere in the background of my living, *someone* is very much afraid, but it does not appear to be me. Does that make any sense to you, my Giobella—my own girl?" He took hold of both her hands again, leaning close to stare into her eyes. "Because it makes no sense at all to me, and it does frighten me. It does."

"No," she said. "No, of course it makes no sense—how can you even ask me that?" Then she smiled, pressing her hands more firmly into his. "But nothing has made sense since the first time I drove Romano's mail van up here and saw you with a pregnant unicorn. Since I fell in love like an idiot, forever in love with a man twice my age, who writes poetry and makes silly jokes, and has a goat named out of an opera." The green eyes darkened, but they held his own eyes without tears. "Who will not lift a finger to save himself from the *'Ndrangheta*, because the unicorn told him it would be all right. Bianchi, I meant what I said—I am *not* coming to your funeral."

"*Va bene, tesora,*" Bianchi said again. "Then I certainly will not come, either."

They went to bed early. This time Bianchi woke, not to the sound of a door being smashed in, nor of heavy boots attempting to treat his ribs in the same way, but to the sensation of cold metal being nudged—oddly gently, considering—just under his nose. He opened his eyes slowly and saw the guns.

Beside him, Giovanna uttered a small squeak, but made no other sound. In the predawn light, he saw that there were many more men than there had been the previous time; enough that some had to crowd into the bedroom doorway and the kitchen beyond. They were large men, for the most part, looking generally like young businessmen whose ventures were not doing well. All of them were holding pistols, and two held kerosene cans— it was that smell that had begun to awaken him, even before the gun barrel in his face.

The only one unarmed was the monster, who stood close to the bed, smiling down at Bianchi. As immaculately dressed as ever, a Toscano between the thumb and forefinger of his right hand, he said, "Signor Bianchi. So sorry to disturb your well-earned slumber."

Bianchi sat up, putting his arm around Giovanna's trembling shoulders. Feeling her fear angered him—*my Giobella is not to be afraid of this pig*—and he demanded, "What do you want?"

The monster sighed, as though their dispute had already gone on too long. "What I wanted before, as I informed you then. What I have always wanted—a quiet little farm, with one or two unicorns on it, to spend my declining years in peace. Would you say that this was too much to ask, Signor Bianchi?"

"There are no unicorns here," Bianchi said. "There were, yes, I admit that, but they are gone. Search as you like." He yawned, and made as though to settle comfortably back in the bed.

The monster smiled benignly again, patting Bianchi's cheek. "Oh, that will not be necessary." He pointed to the window: a very small movement, no more than a flick of two fingers. "Come and see for yourself, if you will."

La Signora and her black colt might have been posing against the dawn, so clearly they stood out in Bianchi's vineyard, where he had seen her first. Raising her head, she looked toward the house, and he had no doubt that she saw, not only the black sedans parked directly before it, but everyone within, and what was being done there. And he knew equally well, and without any illusion of rescue, that it was all no concern of hers. She was a unicorn.

"You cannot capture them," he said. "You can only kill them."

The monster sighed again. "Do you know, once that would have been enough. The horn, the hide . . . the skull itself, either to mount on my wall or to sell for a price never imagined—what else could I have desired? But now that I have seen them, at this distance . . ."

Giovanna spoke for the first time. "You will never lay your smallest finger on them. They would never let anyone like you come near. Or your *teppisti*, either." She jerked her head contemptuously toward the large, silent men who filled the room.

Bianchi gripped her shoulder hard, but the monster only nodded in mournful accord. "Entirely correct, signorina. We by ourselves could never approach such splendid creatures, not for a moment. But *he* can." The finger-flick toward Bianchi was all but unnoticeable.

"Perhaps I could." Bianchi's voice was level and calm. "But you already know that I never will."

The monster was nodding before Bianchi had finished speaking, simultaneously lighting another Toscano from the first, and grinding the original underfoot on the bedroom floor. "*Bene*, let us consider the two options before us. The possibility most to be wished is that you will cooperate fully with my associates and myself in capturing two genuine unicorns—one, really, for each will follow wherever the other is taken. You will be properly compensated for your assistance, and no harm will come to you and the Signorina Muscari—on that, you have my word." He paused, and while his voice did not change, the depthless brown eyes did. "Then there is the far less pleasant option, which

I truly do not like even to consider." The two men with kerosene cans tilted them slightly, and liquid began slowly to splash onto the floor.

Giovanna gave a soft cry of horror; and though she bit back any other sound, Bianchi could see the color leave her face, even in the dimness of the bedroom. The monster gestured sharply, and the men brought the gas cans upright again. "I would not enjoy this. It would make a point, but otherwise it would do neither of us any good. But I will burn this hovel to the ground, with your good selves inside, if I have to, because making my point is just as important to me as any *fottuto* unicorns. Do you understand me?"

The obscenity, in the quiet, cultivated voice, was as shocking as the threat itself. Bianchi said, "Yes," but hardly heard the reply himself. Beside him, without raising her own voice, Giovanna was giving vent to a rich round of Sicilian and Neapolitan curses that followed upon each other as steadily as the beads of a rosary. Bianchi had had no idea that she knew even half of those phrases, and kept her fluency firmly in mind from then on. The monster finally raised a hand, saying, "Impressive, but not an answer. Signor Bianchi?"

"I will go out to the unicorns," Bianchi said. "If I can calm them while your people slink up on them, I will do so. But I will not help you capture them. That you cannot make me do."

"No, I would not have imagined so," the monster replied graciously. "Good. You will go as close as you can to the unicorns, and my men and I will follow at a respectful distance." He smiled widely at Giovanna with something that might even have been real amusement. "The well-spoken and valiant Signorina Muscari will remain here with my friend Paolo." He indicated a man with a bald bullet head and a recently-broken nose—*did I do that?* "Who is quite aware that he will lose any hand—any finger—that he lays on her. I keep my word."

Bianchi got out of bed and groped for his clothes—grateful, in the single glance that passed between him and Giovanna, that she had indeed bought him a pair of well-cut blue pajamas, which he wore even when she was not with him, for the smell of her. The monster courteously turned his back while Bianchi dressed, nodding him toward the door. "All that is required of you is to keep the unicorns' attention as long as you can, and we will do the rest." Bianchi focused more selectively on the guns then, realizing that several of them were oddly and ominously shaped. He shook his head, trying to look more serenely amused than he felt.

"Your tranquilizers will be useless," he said. "It will not matter what I do. Giovanna has already told you this. I am telling you the same thing now, so that you will not blame us afterward."

The monster had turned back to the window, and his voice had abruptly become as cold and pitiless as the *tramontane*. "Quickly, Signor Bianchi. If they decide to disappear again while you are putting on your shoes, I will be greatly displeased."

Bianchi struggled into his old leather coat that no longer seemed to welcome him, as always, but almost to fight with his fear-stiffened arms and shoulders. He looked once more at Giovanna, then to Paolo, who grinned at him with stubby gray teeth. Then he walked out of the house, and the 'Ndrangheta followed, but he did not look back.

The sun had not yet risen, and the chill air made him wish that he had first emptied his bladder, *but I didn't want them to think that I was pissing myself for fear of them.* His animals, even Cherubino, were nowhere to be seen, *God, did they pour kerosene in the barn, too? La Signora* and her colt were still in his vineyard, not grazing, watching him. He walked toward them, thinking *dangerdangerdanger* as loudly as he could, trying to broadcast fear and warning with nothing but his eyes. The 'Ndrangheta stayed well back, as the monster had ordered them to do, but Bianchi heard their footsteps, the soft insect clicking of the tranquilizer guns being loaded and cocked, and the nervous rustling of ropes in the hands of those who held them. Standing well to the side, the girl Silvana, head low, hands twisting together, shamed eyes looking away as he passed. *The 'Ndrangheta are family, always, nothing can be trusted but the blood. I should have thought about Silvana.*

La Signora, watching his approach, studying the men following him, nudged the black colt behind her; otherwise she showed no alarm and made no sound. The monster was moving up ahead of his men, disobeying his own commands. Bianchi never turned his head, but knew whose hunger chilled the back of his neck. The unicorns waited, unmoving.

Coming within reach of *La Signora*, he bowed his head, on an impulse, as he would have been less likely to do before a queen. The unicorn put her head against his, her breath whuffling lightly in his hair. *She smells like autumn, the first morning.* He could hear the whisper of the ropes being shaken out into nooses, and for a single moment he tangled his fingers deep in her mane.

Then he was on her back.

For all that his head slightly topped her shoulder, it felt as though he were clawing his way up the face of a glacier. A cold mist closed on him from the first moment, and sound thinned to indistinguishable chitterings, and to a few somewhat louder noises which might have been either shouts or gunshots. *La Signora* surged under him as he straddled her: not as a single creature, not even as a unicorn, but as something that did not know him, a white vastness that wished him neither evil nor any recognizable good, but only its own immortal freedom and power. He clung with all his strength to the dark-gold mane he could not see, knowing beyond thought that if he fell he would be trampled and gored to dust for his equally vast audacity before ever the 'Ndrangheta laid hands on him. He tried to see Giovanna's face behind his tight-shut eyelids, but the sole image that came to him was the somber devil-face of the old goat Cherubino; and in that never-to-be-confessed moment, he yearned for the slit-pupiled yellow eyes just as deeply and hungrily as for the loving, amused green ones.

Well, you will never see her again, Bianchi, so she will never know.

The unicorn did not rear or buck like a horse, nor whirl in neck-snapping circles to throw him off; rather, she had become the spinning center of a spinning, melting universe, so that he could neither feel the jar of her hooves on the ground, nor be certain where any ground might truly be. Dazed and disoriented, he flattened himself along her neck; and somewhere as far away as Giovanna's eyes, she screamed, and her son echoed her call. And Bianchi heard a third cry—a thin night-bird wail of hopeless terror and loss—and knew it for his own, and despaired. And still he hung on, insane and unyielding, with the unicorn's mane whipping his eyes blind.

Which was perhaps the only way that he could ever have seen *La Signora's* mate coming to her.

Bianchi always remembered the black unicorn as far huger than it could have been, as though somehow magnified a hundred or a thousand times by the mist through which it strode. Its blackness made both the word and the color meaningless: it appeared to him like night folded in midnight and hammered into something resembling a great animal, magnificently grotesque. There was no way that he could have realized it fully: if *La Signora's* beauty was barely comprehensible to human vision, her mate could exist for such vision only as fury. The horn blazed and rippled, pointing across the freezing wind straight at his heart. The eyes beneath were the color of lightning.

"*No,*" Bianchi whispered into the blackness. "No, *Signor . . .*"

He closed his eyes, because the eyes of the black unicorn were too terrible to meet, and flailed his legs as wildly as an infant, struggling to dismount with no assurance that he would not plummet through immortality to shatter like a cheap watch on an earth centuries below. But instead he tumbled no more than two feet, landing erect, though the unexpected impact juddered through all his bones, snapped his teeth on his tongue, and promptly gave him a grinding headache behind his eyes. He lurched forward, but somehow kept his balance and stood swaying, arms out as though he were either trying to keep from falling or yearning after something wonderful and gone. And for the life of him, at that moment Claudio Bianchi could not himself have said which was so.

Nor could he have told where or when he was— or, really, *if* he was—for he seemed completely uncentered, derailed, at right angles to everything he assumed. He was certainly standing in what looked quite a bit like his own vineyard, except that, like all else he saw—his fields, his cow barn, his ancient Studebaker—it had turned a pale, almost colorless gray-green; nor would it stay quite still, but kept shivering faintly in and out of focus . . . unless *he* were the one shifting, blurring, unable to take hold on the world. *Is this what* La Signora *came to tell me, after all? Is this what living looks like to the dead?*

There was no sign of any unicorn. There was no sound to be heard at all, though he saw men of the *'Ndrangheta* seemingly attempting to speak to one another, their movements as impossibly tedious and jerky and *wrong* as even the lines of his own house. Almost all of them kneeling, they huddled in near-transparent gray-green clumps, looking past him, plainly not seeing him at all, but just as definitely staring after *something* . . .

And then he actually felt himself going mad, felt his mind slipping from him like a physical thing, because he saw slaughtered Third Cat, as whole as himself, picking its way delicately toward him, unquestionably recognizing him, ghost to ghost, a fellow gone-away. He said, "No, cat. Pass me by, cat," but could not hear his own voice, nor feel the words in his mouth. "Cat, cat, please . . . pass me by."

The monster lay on his face only a few feet from him, but the space between them seemed as vast to Bianchi's imagining as the desert that the *sirocco* brought to his doorstep every spring. He never knew how long it took him to cross to the dead man's side, to take trembling hold of the elegant topcoat, now splotched and sticky with drying blood, and turn the monster over. *I can touch him, move him, so that must mean that I am not dead, surely?* The broad chest had been split open to the breastbone—*like Third Cat, exactly like my poor Third Cat*—clearly by some immense force, as though some god had been furiously hammering down a railroad spike. The monster's face, however, was unmarked, except by damp earth, and his eyes were wide: not at all with fear, as Bianchi read his expression, but with an almost childlike curiosity. Bianchi closed them.

He began to mumble the few Latin phrases he always spoke at the burial of a farm animal—*there, a ghost could never do that*—but he never finished them. Staring down at the dead face, no Toscano now between the strong white teeth and the courteously contemptuous lips, a rage such as he had never known took hold of him, shaking him between merciless jaws as he had seen a younger Garibaldi shake a poor mouse or blind, helpless mole. He kicked the corpse savagely, trampled it, kicked dirt over it. Every blood vessel in his body, from the least capillary to the great, rolling arteries of the heart, seemed to be swollen with storm beyond his understanding, so that when he cried out it was as much with vast, impossible bewilderment as with pain and fury. He could not hear what he was screaming.

Now he became aware that he was moving forward, toward the gray-green, half-transparent men who were all backing away. Some were pointing at him, or perhaps at Third Cat, who, more sociable than he had ever been in life, stalked beside him, purring silently. "They are afraid of you," Bianchi said. "They should be."

The storm in his body forced his mouth to open, and a voice came out of him that was not his voice. It rang and echoed through him, and made his headache worse, but he noticed in a detached way that it shook the trees.

The other voice said, "A unicorn has been born here. You trespass on sacred land." The figures of the 'Ndrangheta, still unfocused in his sight, kept stuttering in and out of clarity, making him blink constantly, as the other voice grew harsher and more ominous. "Go away. Never come back. Never come back. If you come back, you will be cursed and die. A unicorn has been born here."

They were already straggling away, wobbling windup toys close to running down. The voice in Bianchi's mouth repeated, "Go away. Never come back. You trespass."

Those who stumbled past the dry, unremarkable hollow where Bianchi had brought *La Signora's* son out of her into a rainstorm, gaped over their shoulders at it, often covering their faces, lurching into one another. Bianchi felt his own knees go, and sank down very slowly.

He did not realize that he too had put his hands to his face until he felt the tears.

Dead people cannot cry. I am almost certain of that.

When he opened his eyes, the dislocated world had slipped back into place, though he never sensed any crack or click, as with a bone. Color and sound had returned—he clearly heard the cows lowing to be taken out, heard Garibaldi barking raggedly at an annoying magpie—and the angle of the just-risen sun made him aware that less than an hour had passed since a pistol muzzle had invaded his mustache. Engines were starting up, tires were hissing and spraying stones; harsh voices were shouting shakily back and forth in tremulous anger. Third Cat was gone.

And Giovanna was running toward him from the house, as he had imagined her running through the rain to see *La Signora's* child being born. He got to his feet again and waited for her, feeling very old. When she leaped into his arms, he promptly toppled over; but instead of helping him up, she laughed and rolled in the damp morning grass with him, until Bianchi was forced to push her gently away, laughing himself for what felt like the first time since his childhood. He demanded, "What happened? Giobella, what happened?"

She stared. "Didn't you see? You were . . . you were *riding* her! Why did you . . . what made you. . . ?" She ran out of words, and was reduced to flapping her arms helplessly, while trying simultaneously to hold him. "Bianchi, why are you asking me what happened to you?"

"Because I don't *know!*" He lowered his voice, peering toward the house. "And who, *cazzo di Bacco*, is *that?*"

Giovanna turned her head briefly. "Oh, that is Paolo—you remember him. He would not let me come out to you, so I kicked him." The *'Ndrangheta* who had been sprawled across the doorstep was standing now, but movement was plainly uncomfortable for him. Giovanna called through cupped hands, "Hurry up, Paolo, your friends are all leaving! It will be a long walk home with your *coglioni* in a sling!"

Paolo shot her one weakly murderous glance, and limped away. Giovanna said quietly, "I heard the shots. Three, four, maybe five shots. I pushed Paolo aside, and I ran to the door. You were . . . Bianchi, you were *disappearing!* You were on her back—I just got a little glimpse of you, and you looked so frightened, my insides just . . ." She held him so hard against her breast that for a moment he could not distinguish her heartbeat from his own. "What were you *doing*, Bianchi? Claudio, Claudio, *vita mio*, what were you trying to do? I thought—I thought . . ." Bianchi could not make out the last words.

He said, "I don't know." Mezzanotte and the three-legged cat Sophia came to investigate them, while pretending immense unconcern. "I think I had some notion of riding her very far away from there, before those men could get at her with their ropes and their tranquilizers. It makes no sense, I know . . . but, Giobella, she would not run, she had no *care* for such people. She is so different from us, humans, so much *better* . . ." His voice thickened in his throat. "I think you were right. I think perhaps she was hunted here from some other time. Where they do not have tranquilizer guns."

"They had other things then," Giovanna pushed his head back to look into his face. It was Bianchi's turn to stare back speechlessly. She said, "I saw *him*."

Bianchi had been shaking his head for some time before he found words. "You can't have seen him. *I* never really saw . . . they are not what we see here, down here . . ." He took hold of her hands and pressed their coolness against his closed eyes.

Giovanna whispered, "I saw night. The sun was rising, but I saw night and stars over you . . . terrible stars. I called out to you."

"I called to you," Bianchi said. "Then I fell, like the boy in that Greek story, Icarus. I thought I fell a long way—across the sky, maybe—but I don't know now. Did you see me then?"

"No." Giovanna's body had gone strangely rigid, and her voice was shaking. "Bianchi, I have to ask—are you *you?*"

Bianchi did not reply. Giovanna said, "You rode a unicorn. That's not for people to do—not people like us, never mind the old stories. Maybe you fell from the moon, maybe you fell out of a tree, I don't care, I don't care. But is it . . . is it still you I am holding?" The deep-green eyes seemed as swollen as ripe fruit, close to bursting with hope and sweetness and fear. "After where you've been . . . after what has—I don't know—*happened,* are you still my cranky old Claudio Bianchi? Who . . . who warms my feet?"

Bianchi stood up, lifting her with him. "It's me," he said simply. "No better a man than I ever was, no wiser a soul—and certainly no deeper a poet. If you doubt it, listen." And he recited the last two lines of the poem that had so disappointed him because it kept turning into a kind of testament.

Giovanna Muscari, sitting in the beautiful sun
of a long and beautiful life,
remember that someone called you 'Giobella'

When she had stopped crying, she said, "That is a terrible poem. I am sure the rest of it is just as bad. Only you would have written it." Then she started crying again, and it took him some while to understand what she was whispering. "Bianchi, I saw . . . I saw you with that dead man, what you *did* . . . and then when you were walking, when you went toward those others . . . Bianchi, the sun was behind you, and your shadow . . . it wasn't *your* shadow . . . there was the *horn* . . ."

Bianchi held her. "*Sono io,*" he said, over and over. "*Sono io,* it's me. Whatever you saw, it's only me now."

Cherubino came lolloping up to nose at his pockets, and Garibaldi wriggled out from under the house. Bianchi pretended to wave them off, demanding, "And where were you, my brave defenders, when Giobella and I needed defending? Hah? You should be ashamed!"

Giovanna sniffled, and laughed shakily. "Do not scold them, Claudio. They were afraid of the guns." She buried her face in his damp shoulder again.

The sky was as clear as Bianchi could recall seeing it, and as blue as the pines of the faraway Aspromontes. There were only three clouds to be seen from horizon to horizon. Two were dark, as though with rain; one was a translucent white-gold, as though lighted from within. They were moving away slowly, toward the sunrise.

"No," he said, so softly that Giovanna never heard him. "No. It is over. Those are clouds."

But inside he spoke to the sky, his mind so frayed by exhaustion that he could barely think coherently. *Goodbye. I do not want to watch you leaving, but you believed that I was brave enough to bear your touch, and to see what you are. So now I am as brave as you needed me to be—though no braver than the rest of us who do as we can in this country, even that old thief Falcone—even our senile Madame Leonora. I am glad that you chose my home to have your child—though I must tell you that it has made my life much more complicated than I like. And I am proud that I could be whatever help I have been to you, and I thank you for your shining . . . and for the poems,* but he was looking at Giovanna as he thought the word. *If I never see you again—and I never will—thank you for the poems. Goodbye,* Signora.

Against him, still not looking up, Giovanna said, "And the *'Ndrangheta?* Will your . . . your shadow keep them away?"

"No, I told you, I am only me, no black unicorn. But the land . . . the land will keep them out. It really is sacred now, you know. In a little time, I will be as peacefully alone here as I ever was." He smiled into Giovanna's hair. "More or less."

"I will never come and live with you," she promised. "Not until you ask me. And maybe not even then."

Bianchi turned to look back toward the ravaged vineyard. "*Ay*, so much to do," he muttered. "So much to replant, regrow . . . and how I get the smell of that *piscio* out of the house. . . ?" Then he said, "I wonder how long unicorns stay together."

Giovanna stared at him. "What do you mean?"

"Well, not so many creatures mate for life. I have read about this. Birds, yes, and foxes, and

173

some of the monkeys . . . and some kinds of mice, perhaps . . . and I think even some fish, oh, and maybe wolves. But my cats do not even want the males around, once they know—and DeLorenzo says his sheep—"

"Cats—fish—*sheep*! We are talking about *unicorns*!" She gripped his coat lapels, dragging him close. "They may be apart sometimes, they may come and go as they choose—what can love be like when you live forever?—but they *wait* for each other, they find each other, they are together always! You take your stupid fish and mice back, Claudio Bianchi! I would die if I did not think that they would always be together!"

Bianchi pried her hands from his coat and held them tightly with his own. "Even if they have brothers?" Giovanna blinked in surprise, and then nodded firmly. "Even if one of them is very much older than the other?"

The green eyes met his own steadily, and drew them into a different forest from *La Signora's* eyes. "When you are going to live forever, what difference?"

"Well, then," Bianchi said. "Well, then."